THE RIVER

———

Rumer Godden

Introduced by Anita Desai

virago

VIRAGO

This paperback edition published in 2015 by Virago Press
The River first published in Great Britain in 1946 by Michael Joseph Ltd
'Red Doe' and 'The Little Black Ram' published in 1957
by Macmillan & Co. Ltd

The River copyright © Rumer Godden 1946
'Red Doe' and 'The Little Black Ram' copyright © Rumer Godden 1957
Introduction copyright © Anita Desai 2015

A CIP catalogue record for this book
is available from the British Library.

ISBN 978-1-84408-841-6

Typeset in Goudy by M Rules
Printed and bound in Great Britain by
Clays Ltd, St Ives plc

Papers used by Virago are from well-managed forests
and other responsible sources.

MIX
Paper from
responsible sources
FSC
www.fsc.org   FSC® C104740

Virago Press
An imprint of
Little, Brown Book Group
100 Victoria Embankment
London EC4Y 0DY

An Hachette UK Company
www.hachette.co.uk

www.virago.co.uk

CONTENTS

INTRODUCTION

An image that appears frequently in Rumer Godden's work, both fiction and autobiography – and the line between the two is a fine one – is that of a girl flying a paper kite, as she used to on the flat rooftop of her home in Bengal. In the memoir *Two Under the Indian Sun*, which she wrote with her sister Jon, she remembers:

> To hold a kite on the roller was to hold something alive ... something that kicked in your hand, that pulled up and sang as the string thrilled in the wind. The string went up and up until the kite seemed above the hawks circling in the sky; it linked us with another world, wider, far wider than ours.

The young heroine of *The River* declares, 'If it flies, I shall fly.' In both books the kite is used as a metaphor for childhood and the end of childhood. It might as well stand for her long and extraordinary life.

Rumer Godden was born in 1907 and died in 1998, so her life spanned almost the entire twentieth century. She lived through all its great upheavals – two world wars, the expansion of the British Empire, as well as its collapse –

and through periods of personal joy and success, as well as struggle and betrayal. Throughout, she wrote with exemplary steadfastness. What gave a life, which had been volatile and dramatic, its core of stability, of serenity, even?

Two strands ran through it: one was her childhood in India at a time when the British ruled with a sense of security and the continuity of history; the other was her unwavering conviction of writing as her vocation. Towards the end, a third strand became apparent: a spiritual awareness that grew to a point where she felt able to commit to Catholicism. Throughout the twists and turns of a turbulent life, she retained the inner focus and belief of the child on the rooftop, holding the roller as her paper kite is lifted into the sky, allowing it the freedom of the winds, but maintaining her control.

Her father, Arthur Godden, in what Rumer Godden's biographer Anne Chisholm calls 'the high-Victorian heyday of the Empire', fought in the Boer War and then, bored at the prospect of settling down to life as a stockbroker in London, chose instead to work as an agent in one of the shipping companies based in Calcutta that ran steamers up and down the great rivers of the Gangetic delta. In *Two Under the Indian Sun* his life is described as one of adventure, excitement and a passionate attachment to the landscape of the riverine Bengal that Rumer was to inherit and cherish all her life. She described the childhood she and her three sisters shared at the house in Narayanganj, a small town beside a river, as 'halcyon', painting it in golden light, filling it with flowers and birds and imbuing it with all the comfort and security that could be provided by a large staff of servants – there were fifteen for a family of five. Education was certainly haphazard, provided by their maiden aunt Mary who lived with them, but

Rumer grew up with a deep love of books and reading, which led quite naturally to an aptitude for writing. She first saw her writing in print at the age of twelve, in the Calcutta newspaper the *Statesman*, which confirmed her commitment to the writing life: always an imaginative child, she wrote under a pseudonym, assuming the role of a mother, and offered advice on how to keep children cool in the hot weather.

As the girls grew into adolescents, the Goddens decided to follow the British colonial tradition of taking their children back to England for a more conventional education. In 1920 the girls went with their mother to settle in Eastbourne where they learnt that the life of luxury and comfort they had taken for granted as members of the ruling class in India – the flag that was raised on their house at sunrise and lowered at sunset had them think of their home as Buckingham Palace – was over. Rumer found life in Eastbourne bleak and dreary, and suffered from the rigours of school life, going through as many as five in two years. It was in the last of them, Moira House, a progressive institution run by enlightened women, that the vice principal, Miss Swann, saw her literary talent and encouraged her writing. Swann was a writer herself and an exacting critic, but Rumer trusted her, and turned to her even as an adult for advice. One of the most beneficial exercises she gave Rumer was in précis: she had to reduce the leader of *The Times* to fourteen lines so that not a word was wasted. 'I owe her a tremendous debt,' said Rumer in later life.

No one in the family seems to have considered a university education as the next logical step. Instead, in 1925 their mother took them back to India with trunkfuls of new clothes to launch them in Calcutta society with its parties, dances, polo and riding. Rumer never felt comfortable in that social milieu and in 1927 she returned to London where, knowing she would have to support herself financially, she decided to train as a dancing teacher. She studied for two years and was offered a job on the staff, but instead went back to India to open her own dance school, first in Darjeeling and then in Calcutta. She rented premises in the best neighbourhood in the city and the school proved popular, particularly with the Eurasians of Calcutta. The British rather looked down on it for that very reason and there was gossip, hinting that Rumer must have Indian blood herself. She even received anonymous offensive letters and phone calls. Rumer was genuinely interested in the Eurasian community; her contact with the students and her assistant and pianist taught her much about it. She also did a great deal of research for her second novel, *The Lady and the Unicorn*, which she wrote while 'sitting on the verandah of the school building among the waiting pupils, mothers and ayahs'.

Of course, Rumer still belonged to the expatriate British society, and by this time she was married to Laurence Foster, a stockbroker, sportsman, and a popular figure in the exclusive Tollygunge Club circle. The couple honeymooned in Puri by the sea and nearly sixty years later she wrote a novel, *Coromandel Sea Change*, about an unhappy bride's realisation that she had made a mistake. It wasn't a marriage of minds or sensibilities, as was evident from her family's misgivings. In Calcutta she was expected to take part in Laurence's social life: 'for a while I tasted how beguiling it could be – as long as you stayed on the surface', but she remained critical of it: 'They were still in Britain, adapting their exile to as close a British pattern as they could, oblivious of everything Indian except for their servants.' *The Lady and the Unicorn* was born of this criticism of the common British disdain for Indians and

Eurasians. She had already written a book called *Chinese Puzzle* about a Pekinese dog – she had a lifelong passion for the breed – which was published in 1935 when she was in England awaiting the birth of her daughter. It was not a commercial success but it gave her the opportunity to meet her publisher and agent in London. They had faith in her writing, which she took strength from when she returned to India.

Her third novel, *Black Narcissus*, published in 1939, was her first success – both commercial and critical. It was compared by Arthur Koestler to E. M. Forster's *A Passage to India* (which pleased Rumer, who said it was 'the book that changed my life') and turned into a movie. The film, which was enormously successful, disappointed Rumer but it did give her financial security and confidence.

Her marriage, on the other hand, went badly wrong. Her husband's career as a stockbroker failed and he joined the army, leaving Calcutta. Rumer, alone, took her two daughters to live in a small bungalow amidst the mountains and tea gardens of Darjeeling. This was a quiet, contemplative period of her life. She went for long walks and kept a diary that was later published as *Rungli-Rungliot* (subtitled 'Thus Far and No Further'). Next she went to live on a houseboat in Kashmir which was closer to where Laurence was posted, but his cantonment life and the company of soldiers' wives was no more attractive to her than expatriate society in Calcutta had been. Her marriage was effectively over. She moved to a small, basic cottage she called Dove House on a flowery hillside of streams and orchards.

Ultimately, this idyllic setting proved the scene of the most disturbing drama of her life: after the household fell ill and ground glass was found in the food, she became convinced they were being poisoned by the cook, Siddika. This could not be proved in court and he was acquitted but, ill and fearful, she left the place she had been happy and loved, and it would not be long before she would leave India for good. Many years later she wrote a fictionalised account in *Kingfishers Catch Fire*, which displayed her ability to write of the British in India with both intimate knowledge and a critical eye. The book was compared to Paul Scott's *The Jewel in the Crown* and, once again, to Forster's *Passage to India*. It was much less overtly political than either and its scope was narrower but it was an imaginative reconstruction of the colonial situation. As is evident from her novels, which often feature narrow-minded British characters, Rumer had ambiguous feelings about imperialism, but when Prime Minister Jawaharlal Nehru was quoted as saying 'My quarrel with the British is that they left a land of poverty-stricken wrecks,' she rose up in its defence and in 1944/45 she worked on a non-fiction book of the Women's Voluntary Service in Bengal, touring the various organisations it ran, and wrote with admiration of the good work it did.

One of these tours took her back to Narayanganj and, on seeing her old home, was moved to write a short autobiographical novel called *The River*. On reading it, the French director Jean Renoir immediately bought film rights, describing it as 'exactly the type of novel which would give me the best inspiration for my work ... an unexpressed, subtle, heartbreaking innocent love story involving a little girl.' They began a correspondence and Rumer helped him plan a trip with his wife to the site. On their return, he invited Rumer to Hollywood so they could work on the script together. 'Working with Jean was the best and richest year I've spent,' she later said. So different in character and background, the two became very close and held each other in high regard.

Staying with the Renoirs, she met their friends the Chaplins, the Stravinskys, James Mason, Charles Laughton, Elizabeth Taylor and Greta Garbo, and hugely enjoyed the social life. When the script was ready to be filmed, she accompanied the crew to Bengal, sharing many decisions with the director. The film was shown at the Venice Film Festival in 1951 and won the International Critics' Prize, then opened in France and the USA to good reviews and is now regarded as a classic. Although the Indian press was rather critical of it, it had a premiere at the New Empire cinema in Calcutta that was attended by Prime Minister Nehru. Many of Godden's books were made into successful films in her lifetime, including Powell and Pressburger's famous adaptation of *Black Narcissus*; *Enchanted*, starring David Niven, which was based on *A Fugue in Time*; *The Battle of the Villa Fiorita*; *The Greengage Summer*; and *In this House of Brede*, but none of them brought her the satisfaction of *The River*.

Rumer divorced Laurence Foster, creating some turmoil for her daughters – which she later fictionalised in *The Battle of the Villa Fiorita* – and after filming *The River* she entered into a second, and very happy, marriage to James Haynes-Dixon, a civil servant who devoted himself to her and her career. Together they created a series of beautiful homes and gardens in London and in the countryside, including Lamb House in Rye, which was once the home of Henry James; her surroundings had always been very important to her.

In 1961 she made a new friend in Dame Felicitas Corrigan of Stanbrook Abbey in Worcestershire, and through her she established a link with the Benedictine order that led to her writing *In This House of Brede*, her longest, perhaps most complex novel, in which she strove to realistically depict convent life: many of the events were inspired by the nuns' own stories. In 1973 her husband died and a few years later she moved to a small house next to her daughter Jane's in Scotland, but she continued to write with her old regularity and determination. It was her habit to start a new book every New Year's Eve and in her lifetime she completed an astonishing twenty-three novels, twenty-six books for children, fourteen books of non-fiction and seven collections and anthologies of poetry. In 1993 she was awarded the OBE.

This was not to be retirement for her. In 1994 the BBC planned a documentary on her life for the *Bookmark* programme and she was persuaded to travel with them to India for the last time for the making of the film. She returned to Bengal and even to Kashmir where she had sworn never to go again. It was an exhausting undertaking but at a farewell dinner she toasted the crew and told them that if she were a sensible old lady she would not have agreed to the journey and that she was glad she 'had never been sensible in her life'. She died four years later at the age of ninety and was buried next to her husband James in the old cemetery in Rye.

Rumer Godden knew both success and popularity in her life. Perhaps for that very reason she was troubled that she might be considered not a very serious but an entertaining, lightweight writer. She was also conscious of her own attractions to the whimsical and the precious, and the need to be on her guard and reserve that aspect for her many charming books for children. She never lost the child's fascination with the miniature but if there is any criticism that this prevented her from addressing the large events and political movements of her time, it does not hold; the miniature in her books contained, by reflection, the vastness of the world. This is surely the reason why her work has given so much pleasure to generations in many lands, and continues to do so.

Perhaps no other book exemplifies Rumer Godden's strengths as well as this little book, barely over a hundred pages long. In her modest way, she herself seemed bemused by how well it was received when it was published, in 1946, and how it caught the eye of the French director Jean Renoir, who turned such unlikely material into an acclaimed film.

As in her other work, she does not directly refer to the Second World War, the time in which it is set. In fact, the young heroine, labouring over the Latin declension for war, thinks 'this war, the last war, any war, it does not matter which war.' Nor is there a reference to the struggle for freedom that cumulated a year later in India's independence and the end of the colonial empire. Yet it is imbued with a sense of time passing, of time being a river that never stands still, and the seasons that change inexorably from one to another.

These are profound intimations, all the more intense because they are perceived by a child. Harriet's world is a square grey-stucco house occupied by her family – parents, an older and a younger sister, a small brother – and the large domestic staff that serves them: the gatekeeper who makes time to play games with the children, the wise and practical Nan, and the many who bring the different religious beliefs and customs with them – Hindu, Muslim, Buddhist and Christian. Whatever the children learn of India and its diversity is through them. The outside world is the street beyond the walls with its bazaar life going on, and beyond that the river, with its steamers, sailing boats and ferries moving up and down it. A small area on a map, but Rumer Godden conveys an immense sense of space:

the sky where birds wheel and paper kites fly; the river with its constantly moving kingfishers and porpoises; the garden with its teeming plant and insect life, minutely observed by the little boy Bogey, for whom it holds endless fascination.

In this seemingly safe and secure setting, the children live what might be thought an idyllic existence, but it is within its confines that Harriet finds herself thinking, in bewilderment, 'children don't have loves and wars. Or do they ... of their kind?' In a very real way, a serpent too inhabits this Garden of Eden, and the child who had been innocent learns of the existence of evil.

These events, or non-events, are written of with an artlessness, a spontaneity that make one think they must have flowed from her memory through her pen on to paper with the ease of running water. Actually, Rumer Godden wrote and rewrote these scenes but seemed unable to bring them together. It was when she revisited India on an assignment from the Women's Voluntary Service in Bengal that she was inspired to write it. During her research, one of her tours took her to Narayanganj, where she had lived as a child: 'As I walked through the bazaars and Jute works, along the river, past the Club, the bamboo-built church and school, the houses I had known, it was as if I had gone back ... seven, eight, nine, ten, eleven, twelve years ... again. Everything was the same.' She left by steamer and from its deck watched the town 'grow smaller but more and more clear until out of sight.' Out of this moment of clarity the final version of *The River* was born: she had discovered how to capture time, space and experience in exquisite miniature, no more than a dewdrop reflecting light.

Anita Desai, 2014

THE RIVER

PREFACE

There is a vast difference between a book that is 'vouch-safed', its idea or theme coming of itself into your mind, and a book that comes from searching for a story or plot that fits the idea that is in your mind. *The River* was one of those rare books that are given to you.

Jean Renoir, the great French film director, who made the exquisite film of *The River*, called the book 'a tribute to India and to childhood'; which I suppose it is – to my own childhood, though I never had a small brother who was killed by a cobra.

In my young days all English people living and work-ing in the East, except those who were very poor or very wise, sent their children back to England to be brought up, even though this meant years of separation during which the children were exiles. We, my sister Jon and I, were two small English girls; India was where our father worked, and we lived there until we were left with our grandmother in London, far from our home. Then suddenly, in 1914, we were fetched back, reprieved.

I was only seven but realized, as soon as we were back, how homesick I had been. Jon too. Perhaps the thing we had missed more than anything else was the dust: the feel of the sunbaked Indian dust between sandals and bare toes; that and the smell. It was the honey smell of the fuzz-buzz flowers of thorn trees in the sun, and the smell of open drains and urine, of coconut oil on shining black human hair, of mustard cooking oil and the blue smoke from cowdung used as fuel; it was a smell redolent of the sun, more alive and vivid than anything in the West, to us the smell of India.

In the background of our house at Narayanganj in Bengal – now Bangladesh – there were always three sounds: the regular puff of escaping steam from the Jute Works across the road, puff – wait – puff like the pulse of our days and nights; then, from first daylight until dusk, the cawing of crows in the garden and, all day and most of the night, the tympany of the bazaar: a chatter like sparrows, street cries, a woman wailing, a baby's cry.

Sometimes there was a light rhythmic drumming which meant the monkey man was passing: he always had two performing monkeys dressed up as a man and a woman; the servants used to gather round them and not let us see what they were laughing at. There were other intermittent noises: the Jute Works noise of trucks pushed by hand, of presses working, chantings of coolies as they pushed or moved some heavy truck or piece of machinery, of bellows and of iron hitting iron from the forge. River noises came: the whistle of a launch, the deep hoot announcing a steamer. Every now and then there was a near and immediate noise of jarring, which meant the big gates of the house were being rolled open by the gatekeeper; it was always an exciting noise, heralding an arrival; all those noises are still there.

The gates were high and green, made of solid wood for privacy, under an arch of bridal creeper that canopied them with a cloud of green and white. On the garden side was the gatekeeper's lodge, a small cell built into the wall; in the left-hand gate a door was cut through which servants or peons went in and out but, for any of the family, even for a child coming back from a ride on her pony, the full panoply was gone through, the gates rolled open with a rumble that alerted the whole house.

A wide gravelled drive made a half circle round an enormous cork tree, whose feathery green reached as high as the roof parapet; in December it burst into a tent of white blossom and had round its foot a bed of amaryllis lilies with red streaked trumpets. I called it my tree. Lawns spread away on either side. On the left was a glimpse of a tennis court with screens of morning glory.

I suppose it was a monstrous house, a great rectangle of pale grey stucco, standing on a high plinth that was hidden by plumbago and a hedge of poinsettias – it has always seemed strange to us that in England, for Christmas, poinsettias are sold singly at large prices. Verandahs, stone arched and green shuttered, ran the full length of the two floors, each arch ornamented with white carving. The roof was flat, with a high parapet which was cut into loopholes. Double steps, banked with pots of budding chrysanthemums, led up from the drive.

Narayanganj's river was the Lakya, part of the vast network of the Brahmaputra, and was the only direct way in to the town; a branch line railway ran to Dacca, Bengal's capital – now called Dhaka – eleven miles away and, going to Dacca too, was a road built high on a bund above the jute and rice fields, but these were only side routes: the main traffic was by river.

All my young life was lived on or by Indian rivers and was concerned with tides and weather warnings, with steamers, launches, flats, motor-boats, any kind of boats. Rivers of European countries were pygmies to these Indian rivers; they were often two miles wide, flowing between banks of mud and white sand from which fields stretched flat to the horizon under a weight of sky. If we children grew up with a sense of space in us, it was from the sky.

I left India – at least living there – in 1945, immediately after the Second World War. In my last winter – cold weather as we called it – I was asked to do a report for the Women's Voluntary Services on what British women were doing in the way of war work; derogatory questions had been raised in Parliament. I was told to choose a province, so chose Bengal which I knew best and which allowed me to be in and out of Calcutta where Jon could look after the children. I travelled unobtrusively, wearing every kind of uniform so that people took me for granted; the result was a book, *Bengal Journey*.

As part of the journey I had to go from Dacca to Narayanganj, driving along the road that was utterly familiar to me.

My hostess-to-be at Narayanganj had telephoned early

that morning; the manager of one of the Jute Works that spread on both banks of the river had died and was to be buried that morning as is the custom in a hot country – it was April – and, of course, every European in Narayanganj's small community had to drive into Dacca to attend the funeral. As I was booked to leave on the midday steamer for Calcutta it was impossible to postpone my visit and, 'Would you mind,' she asked, 'being received by the babu (Indian clerk) in charge?' Mind! I could not have been more relieved but had no idea of what was waiting for me.

Indians do not change; their clothes and customs are timeless and there was not one Westerner in the little town to disturb this. As I walked through the bazaars and the Jute Works, along the river, past the Club, the bamboo-built church and school, the houses I had known, it was as if I had gone back thirty or more years and was – seven, eight, nine, ten, eleven, twelve – again. Everything was the same: I had lunch on the verandah of one of the houses, waited on by white-clad servants who might have been our own. On the way to the ghat, we passed the gates of our house; I could see the top of my cork tree over the gate. A short way up its trunk was a hole, my secret hole where I kept the poems I wrote and showed to no one else but Jon. For a moment I hesitated. 'Go in. Go in,' the babu urged but I could not bring myself to do that.

Most uncanny of all was the steamer; it was one of my father's double-decked paddle-wheeled steamers – Fa was in the Inland Navigation Company of India – with the first class forward on the upper deck, where I was the only passenger. As the paddle wheels began to turn I stood at the front rail.

Usually, as I knew well, the steamers drew away from the ghat, then turned in a wide circle to go upstream but now, for some reason, the steamer backed. She backed further and further so that I, looking at the town, its banks along the river, its houses, mosques, temples and bathing steps, saw it grow smaller and smaller until it was like looking at it down a telescope, smaller but more and more clear until it was out of sight.

As the steamer turned I went to my cabin and began to write *The River*.

The river was in Bengal, India, but for the purpose of this book, these thoughts, it might as easily have been a river in America, in Europe, in England, France, New Zealand or Timbuctoo, though they do not of course have rivers in Timbuctoo. Its flavour would be different in each; Bogey's cobra would, of course, have been something else and the flavour of the people who lived by the river would be different.

That is what makes a family, the flavour, the family flavour, and no one outside the family, however loved and intimate, can share it. Three people had the same flavour as the child, Harriet, who lived in this garden; were her contemporaries, her kin; Bea was one, the others were Bogey and Victoria. They lived in their house beside the river, in a jute-pressing works near a little Indian town; they had not been sent away out of the tropics because there was a war; this war, the last war, any war, it does not matter which war.

It is strange that the first Latin declension and conjunction should be of love and war:

Bellum	Amo
Bellum	Amas
Bellum	Amat
Belli	Amamus
Bello	Amatis
Bello	Amant

'I can't learn them,' said Harriet. 'Do help me, Bea. Let's take one each and say them aloud, both at once.'

'Very well. Which will you have?'

'You had better have love,' said Harriet.

In the heat they both had their hair tied up on top of their heads in topknots, but Bea wore a cerise ribbon; the effect of it on her topknot gave her a geisha look that was interesting and becoming. Her eyebrows, as she studied this Latin that it was decreed that they should learn, were like fine aloof question marks.

'Do you *like* Latin, Bea?'

'No, of course I don't, but if I have to learn it,' said Bea, 'it is better to learn it quickly.' She glanced across at Harriet. 'You are always trying to stop things happening, Harriet, and you can't.'

But Harriet still thought, privately, that she could.

It was the doldrums of the afternoon and Bea and

Harriet, the older children, had to do their homework, opposite one another, at the dining-room table. It was hot. Outside the garden was filled with hot, heavy, sleepy sun; there was a smell of leaves and grass and of sun on the house stone. Beyond the garden was the sound of the river and from far away came a whoop from Bogey. I wonder what Bogey has found now, thought Harriet, and wriggled. The fan blew on her forehead, but it only blew hot air, the polish of the table was sticky and held the skin of her arms, there was a dusty dry feeling of dust between her toes. 'You will get hookworm, Harriet, if you go barefoot,' Nan told her. 'Why do you? Bea doesn't.' Harriet looked now under the table to see. No, Bea's feet were gracefully crossed in their correct sandals.

'You had better get on, Harry,' said Bea. 'You have algebra to do as well, and music, and you haven't learnt your Bible verses yet. Better hurry, Harriet.'

Harriet sighed. Latin, and algebra, and music and other things: eating liver, having an injection, seeing a mad paidog – how did Bea manage to take them all so quietly? How? Harriet sighed. She could not, nowadays, aspire to Bea.

'Nan, why is Bea so different?'

'She always was,' said Nan.

'No, she is changing.'

'She is growing up,' said Nan. 'We all have to, willy-nilly.' Harriet did not much like the sound of that expression, 'willy-nilly'.

'Oh, well!' she said, and sighed again and her mind went off on a rapid Harriet canter of its own, too rapid for stops. Will-I-get-hookworm-you-get-all-kinds-of-worms-in-India-and-diseases-too-there-is-a-leper-in-the-bazaar-no-nose-and-his-fingers-dropping-off-him-if-I-had-no-fingers-I-couldn't-learn-music-could-I-no-March-of-the-Men-of-Harlech. She looked at her own fingers, brown and small and whole, except that one had a nail broken where Bogey had banged it, and one had a scratch new that morning, and two were stained bright yellow from the dye she had been making from the yellow flower of a bush that grew beside the cook-house.

The middle finger of Harriet's right hand had a lump on the side of it; that was her writing lump; she had it because she wrote so much, because she was a writer. 'I am going to be a poet when I grow up,' said Harriet; and she added, after another thought, 'Willy-nilly.' She kept a private diary and a poem book hidden in an old box that also did as a desk in an alcove under the side-stairs, her Secret Hole, though it was not secret at all and there was no need to hide her book because she could not resist reading her poems to everyone who would listen. Sometimes she carried her book pouched in her dress. She was writing a poem now, and, as she began to think of it, her eyes grew misty and comfortable.

> *'Saw roses there that comforted her heart*
> *And saw their crimson petals plop apart.'*

'*Plop* apart?' asked Bea, her eyebrows more clear and more surprised and Harriet blushed. She had not known she had spoken aloud.

'*Do* get on, Harry.'

'Yes, Bea – *Amo, Amas, Amat . . . Bellum . . . Belli . . . Bello . . .*'

War and love. How many children, wondered Harriet, yawning, had had to learn those since – she cast round in her mind for someone prominent who could have learnt them – since Julius Caesar, say, or Pontius Pilate (they must have learnt them, they were Romans) or even Jesus – perhaps-if-Jesus-went-to-school. She yawned again and reached for the Outline of History. Loves-and-Wars, she thought, flipping over the pages. Xerxes-Alexander-Goths-and-Huns – Arthur-and-Guinevere-

RichardtheLionheart-Marlborough-Kitchener. Love and war, love and hate all muddled up together. She remembered she had no history to prepare; it was Bible verses and she shut up the book and opened Father's old Bible that they used for lessons. Ever-since-AdamandEve, cantered off Harriet, Cain-Abel-Jacob LeahandRachel-the-Children of Israeland-all-the-rest-of-them. Even in stories, even in plays, and she looked at Bea's elbow holding down the edges of the Shakespeare's flimsy pages that blew up under the fan. Shylock and Portia-and-RomeoandJuliet-and-Cleopatra. She liked Cleopatra best, but even thinking of Cleopatra she wondered that no one ever grew tired of it, of all this love and all this war. Or if they do, she thought, someone starts it all over again. It is as much life as living, thought Harriet. You are born, you are a he or a she, and you live until you die ... Willy-nilly. Yes. Nan is right. It all *is* willy-nilly, though I think you could live very well without a war ... and I suppose without being loved. But I hope I am loved, thought Harriet, as much as Cleopatra, and she thought, I wish I were not so young ... children don't have loves or wars. She drew circles on her algebra. Or do they? wondered Harriet. Do they ... of their kind?

A drum began to beat softly in the village behind the house. Harriet sat up. 'Bea. Tonight is Diwali.'

'I know. But if you haven't done your homework,' Bea pointed out, 'you won't be allowed to go.'

Bea loved Diwali night as much as Harriet did, but when she was excited, she managed to contain her excitement as she contained her likes and dislikes. How? Harriet gave her another long look and sank back baffled. 'I thought you had forgotten,' she said.

'How could I forget?' said Bea. 'Listen to the drums.'

All day the drummers had been going round the town and the villages that lay around it. Diwali was the Hindu festival of the Feast of Lights.

There are ritual festivals in every religion throughout the year, and every family keeps those it needs, the Chinese and the Roman Catholics being perhaps the most elaborate in theirs, though the old Russians and the Hindus come close and Tibet has charming holidays of its own. Diwali was a curious festival to find in the keeping of a European family, but in Harriet's, as in every large household in India, there was always someone who had to keep some one of the different festivals as they occurred: Nan was a Catholic; Abdullah, the old butler, was a Mohammedan, and so was Gaffura his assistant; Maila, the

17

bearer, was a Buddhist from the State of Sikkim; the gardeners were Hindu Brahmins, Heaven Born; the sweeper and the Ayah were Hindu Untouchables and Ram Prasad Singh, the gateman, the children's friend, was of the separate sect of Sikh. Now the gardeners were away in the bazaar, buying the little saucer earthenware festival lamps and the wicks and oil to float in them, while Abdullah and Maila were not interested. The children kept Diwali because it is an irresistible festival and no one could live in the country in which it is held and not be touched by it.

Tonight when it is dark, thought Harriet, her eyes anywhere but on her work, Ram Prasad will have bought for us a hundred or two hundred lamps. They are made of earthenware, shaped like hearts or tarts or leaves, and they cost two pies each (a pie is a third of a farthing), and in each we shall put oil and float a wick; then we shall set them all along the roof and at the windows and in rows on the steps and at the gate and over the gate, and we shall light them. Everywhere, on every house, there will be lights, and on the river the boats will have them burning and we shall see them go past, and other lights on rafts will be floated down and the rich Hindus will give feasts and feed the poor and let off fireworks and we shall stay up to dinner to see.

Diwali, to the children, was also the official opening of the winter. The greenfly came, millions of insects that flew around the lights at dusk. The gardeners began to plant out vegetables and flower seeds. There was a coolness in the mornings and evenings, a thicker dew, more mosquitoes. Then Diwali came, and it was winter. Winter, the cold weather. That is the best time of all, thought Harriet with relish. It seemed to her, as she looked forward to it, a pageant of pleasantness. Soon we shall have fires, thought Harriet, and sweet peas. I wonder what we shall do this winter? What will happen? And as people far wiser than Harriet have thought, she answered herself. Nothing. Nothing at all. Nothing ever happens here. And then she asked Bea, across the table, 'Bea. Is Captain John coming tonight?'

Bea raised her head. 'I suppose he is,' said Bea, and she added uncertainly, 'Bother.'

'Yes. Bother,' said Harriet. 'Bother! Bother! Bother!'

'We must have a quiet winter this year,' Mother had said. 'The world is too unhappy for anything else. There are hurt men and women, and children dying of hunger . . .'

'Oh, Mother!' said Harriet, wriggling.

'Yes,' said Mother firmly, 'think of Captain John.'

'I don't want to think of Captain John,' said Harriet with a feeling of fixed hard naughtiness. 'Why should there be a Captain John?' she asked angrily. 'Or if there must be, why should he want to come here?'

Captain John had come because he had to try to pick up again the threads of living and of earning his living. He had been a prisoner of war and escaped, only to go for more than a year to hospital. He had been tortured in the prison camp, but he was wounded before he went there. He was a young man, or had been a young man, but now his stiff grey face was any age; he had a stiff body, one leg was amputated at the hip, and he had a heavy artificial one that made him more jerky still. The children were warned to be careful of what they said to him. He eschewed grown-ups, but he seemed to like to come into the nursery. Why does he, wondered Harriet. What does he want? He seemed to want something. To be hungry. For what? At first he liked Victoria best, and this was surprising to Harriet because Victoria treated him in a matter-of-fact, offhand way, that was shocking.

'You mustn't, Victoria,' Harriet told her. 'Captain John was *so* brave. He stayed there in the battle until his leg was shot off.'

Victoria's brown eyes rested thoughtfully on Captain John. 'Why didn't he stay until the other leg was shot off?' she asked.

But he still seemed to like Victoria best.

'Did Victoria ask him to come tonight?' said Harriet now. 'Or did Mother?'

There was a silence, and then: 'No one asked him,' said Bea. 'He asked me.'

'*Asked* you?' said Harriet. 'But ...' She had thought that grown-up people did not ask for things.

'He seemed to want to come,' said Bea.

Harriet stared across the table, but all she could see of Bea's face was her forehead and the withdrawn sealed look of her lids as she studied her book. The shadow of her ribbon made a mark of shadow, like a moth, on her cheek. She had withdrawn even further into herself than usual.

Harriet's river was a great slowly flowing mile-wide river between banks of mud and white sand, with fields flat to the horizon, jute fields and rice fields under a blue weight of sky. 'If there is any space in me,' Harriet said, when she was grown up, 'it is from that sky.'

The river emptied itself, through the delta, into the Bay of Bengal, its final sea. There was life in and over its flowing; an indigenous life of fish, of crocodiles and of porpoises that somersaulted in and out of the water, their hides grey and bronze and bubble-blue in the sun; rafts of water hyacinths floated on it and flowered in the spring. There was a traffic life on the river; there were black-funnelled, paddle-wheeled mail steamers that sent waves against the bank and other steamers towing flat jute barges; there were country boats, wicker on wooden hulls, that had eyes painted on their prows and sets of tattered sails to put up in the wind; there were fishing boats, crescents lying in the water, and there were fishermen with baskets, wading in the shallows on skinny black legs, throwing fine small nets that brought up finger-length fishes shining in the mesh. The fish were part of the traffic, and each part was animated by a purpose of its own, and the river bore them all down on its flow.

The small town was sunk in the even tenor of Bengali life, surrounded by fields and villages and this slow river. It had mango groves and water tanks, and one main street with a bazaar, a mosque with a white dome and a temple with pillars and a silver roof, the silver made of hammered-out kerosene tins.

Harriet and the children knew the bazaar intimately;

they knew the kite shop where they bought paper kites and sheets of thin exquisite bright paper; they knew the shops where a curious mixture was sold of Indian cigarettes and betel nut, pan, done up in leaf bundles, and coloured pyjama strings and soda water; they knew the grain shops and the spice shops and the sweet shops with their smell of cooking sugar and ghee, and the bangle shops, and the cloth shop where bolts of cloth showed inviting patterns of feather and scallop prints, and the children's dresses, pressed flat like paper dresses, hung and swung from the shop fronts.

There was only one road. It was built high among the fields so that the monsoon floods would not cover it; it went through villages and sprawling bazaars, and over humpbacked bridges, past bullock carts and walking people and an occasional car. It stretched across country, with the flat Bengal plain rolling to the horizon and clumps of villages, built up like the road, in mounds of mango, banana and coconut trees. Soon the bauhinia tress would bud along the road, their flowers white and curved like shells. Now the fields were dry, but each side of the road was water left from the flood that covered the plain in the rains; it showed under the floating patches of water hyacinth, and kingfishers, with a flash of brilliant blue, whirred up and settled on the telegraph wires, showing their russet breasts.

The river came into view from the road, its width showing only a line of the further bank, its near bank broken with buildings and patches of bazaar and high walls and corrugated-iron warehouses and mill chimneys. Small boats, covered in wicker-work cowls, put out from one bank to ferry across to the other. In boats like that the children went fishing for pearls. The pearls were sunset river pearls, but it was the divers, not the children, who found them; the children could not get their hooks to go deep enough; the divers dived naked to the river-bed.

The children lived in the Big House of the Works. The Works were spread away from the bazaar along the river with the firm's houses and gardens on the further side. The life of every family is conditioned by the work of its elders; think of a doctor's house, or a writer's, a musician's or a missionary's. It is necessary for the whole family to live in the conditions that such work brings; for these children it was jute.

The jute grew in the fields; they knew all its processes: from the seed which their father germinated and experimented with at the Government Farm, through its young growth, when they could not ride their ponies across country, to the reaping and steeping in the water along the road, in dykes along the fields, when its stench would hang over the whole land. They saw it come in on country boats, on bullock carts, into the Works and the piles of it lying in the sheds for carding and cleaning and grading, while the great presses went up and down and the bales were tumbled out of them, silky and flaxen with a strong jute smell. They saw it go away to the steamers; the steamers and flats were piled high with it and took it down the river to the mills of Calcutta.

The sound of the Works came over the wall: the noise of trucks running on their tracks, wagons pushed by hand by brown, sweating coolies, of the presses working and of machinery and the sound of bellows and iron on iron from the foundry, and the clang of the weighing points, the shouting of the tally clerks, the bumping down of the bales and always the regular puff of escaping steam, puff-wait-puff; it was like a pulse in the background of the children's lives. In the inner dimness of the press-rooms was the sheen of the press-tubes, of brass locks, going down with the pale shining heaps of jute that came up again as bales. There was a smell there of jute dust and coal, steam and hot oil and human sweat, that was one of the accompanying smells of their childhood, like the smell of cess and incense and frying ghee in the bazaar and of honey from the mustard and radish flowers when they were out in the fields, and in season, the stench of steeping jute. There were thousands of coolies in the Works, though they were as impersonal as ants to the children. (Bogey used to eat ants to make him wise.) In the concrete-built, double-floored offices there were scores of clerks, babus, in white muslin shirts and dhoties; the children used sometimes to go with their mother to visit the babus' wives and they were given coconut shredded with sugar and 'sandesh', a toffee stuck with silver paper. The firm had its own fleet of launches, called after Indian birds: the 'Osprey', the 'Hoopoe', the 'Oriole', the 'Cormorant', the 'Snipe'; each had its own crew. There were porters or peons, with yellow turbans and staves to guard the gates.

Beyond the Works was the White House, where the Senior Assistant lived, and the Red House where the Junior Assistants all lived together, and the Little House where the Engineer lived. They stood in their own gardens beside the Big House garden.

Other firms were scattered up and down the river, and to them assistants came, young men from England and

Scotland, usually from Scotland, even from Greece, who came out raw and young to learn the trade and ended up as magnates. Later on, they married, and too often, Father said, their wives ended up as magnums.

There were a few other Europeans in the town: a Deputy Commissioner, Mr Marshall, and a doctor, Dr Paget. Once there had been a cantonment, but now all that was left of it was a row of graves in the small European cemetery, where grew trees with flowers like mimosa balls. One grave was of a boy, Piper John Fox, who died nearly two hundred years ago when he was fourteen years old.

Perhaps the place and the life were alien, circumscribed, dull to the grown-ups who lived there; for the children it was their world of home. They lived in the Big House in a big garden on the river with the tall flowering cork tree by their front steps. It was their world, complete. Up to this winter it had been completely happy.

Half of Harriet wanted to stay as a child; half wanted to be a grown-up. She often asked, 'What shall I do when I am? What will it be like?' She often asked the others, 'What shall you be when you are grown up?' It was always Harriet who started these discussions. No one else really liked them except Victoria, who was too young to know what she was, even now.

'I shall be a cross red nurse when I grow up,' said Victoria.

'She means a Red Cross Nurse,' said Nan.

What shall I be? thought Harriet, fascinated. There seemed to her to be infinite possibilities. 'I might be a nun,' she said, 'or a missionary perhaps, then I could help people. Or a doctor. It would be wonderful to be a doctor, to save people's lives, and give your own life up.' The vista was exciting. 'Wonderful,' said Harriet. 'Wouldn't you like that, Bea?'

'No,' said Bea. 'I want my life for myself.'

Harriet was too truthful to deny that she did too, and she tore herself away from the thought of being a doctor. 'So many grown-up people seem to be nothing very much,' she said. She was thinking of the people she knew, of Nan and Father and Mother and Dr Paget and Captain John. They are nothing important, thought Harriet, wondering. Why? They did not seem to mind. But I want to be important. I will be. 'Perhaps I shall be a great dancer,' she said aloud, 'or a politician and make speeches.'

'I thought you were going to be a poet,' said Bea.

'Well . . . I am a poet,' said Harriet.

'You will be what you are. You will have to be,' said Nan, who was unconcernedly darning. 'In the end everyone is what they are.'

'But how shall I know?' cried Harriet, chafing.

'You will find out as you grow,' said Nan, running her needle in and out of the sock stretched on her hand. That seemed altogether too slow for Harriet.

'Bea, what will you be? An actress? Or a hospital nurse? Or a doctor? A great doctor? When you are grown up, what will you be?'

'How can I tell till I get there?' asked Bea.

'But say. You must say. You must be something.'

'I shall wait till I am,' said Bea, tolerantly, 'and then be it.'

'That is a funny sort of answer,' said Harriet, disgusted.

'It is rather a good one,' said Nan.

Harriet found her family maddening. Father was too busy, in a general family and office way, to have any special time to spare for Harriet, or for any of them; Mother was busy, too, with the house, the family, the servants, notes and letters and lessons and accounts; and besides, she was having another baby soon and had not to be disturbed. Nan? Well, Nan was Nan, and to Harriet that was like bread, too everyday and too necessary to be regarded, though she was the staff of life. There used to be Bea, but now Bea was different; she had withdrawn from Harriet; she was quiet, altogether elderly and distant, and she had new predilections; for instance, she had made friends with Valerie from across the river, a big, hard girl, whom Harriet disliked and feared, and who switched Bea away with secrets and happenings in which Harriet had no part. She was no longer sure of Bea. Harriet would have liked to play with Bogey. Though he was much younger, she was young, too, in streaks, but Bogey played in his own Bogey way that was not at all Harriet's. Harriet could never leave anything alone, and Bogey liked things to be alive and behave themselves in their own way. For instance, he played with lizards and grass snakes; he played armies with insects. He did not like toy soldiers. 'They are all tin,' he said. 'I play soldiers with n'insecks.'

'But can't you pretend, Boge?' asked Harriet.

'No, I can't,' said Bogey. 'I like live n'insecks best.'

He was a very thin little boy, with thin arms and legs; his hair was cut short and his forehead showed sensitive and lumpy, while his eyes were small and brown and quick and live. He was absorbed in a completely happy and private life of his own, and though he occasionally needed Harriet, it was seldom for long. His best game was 'going-round-the-garden-without-being-seen', and that hid him even from her. He was always being stung or bruised or bitten, but he managed to contain his wounds as Bea did her difficulties. 'You will get into trouble one of these days,' said jealous, discontented Harriet, but he only smiled and she sensed that he preferred to get into his own trouble himself. It was no good. It was just not possible to play with Bogey.

In her loneliness, Harriet was driven to adopt places; there was her cubbyhole under the stairs, and there was a place on the end of the jetty, the landing-stage by the house. Harriet liked to sit on the end of it, her legs hanging down, her back warmed with sun, her ears filled with the cool gurgling of the water against the jetty poles.

'How is it a Secret Hole when it isn't a secret and it isn't a hole?' Valerie asked about the Secret Hole, but it still felt secret to Harriet, though she used the jetty for her more open thoughts. The flowing water helped her thoughts to flow. She had also, though she did not yet understand about this, an affinity with the cork tree. It was her tree, as the brilliant jacaranda trees, the bamboos and the lace tangles of bridal creeper in the garden, belonged to Bea, and the tight Marechal-Neil rosebuds were Victoria's. Why? She did not know, but she liked to go to the cork tree, she liked to look up into it and if she really wanted to hear the river, she went to listen to it there. There it was not too loud, too near, drawing Harriet, drawing her away as it did on the jetty. Under the cork tree, she could hear it running steadily, calmly and with it, always, the puff-steam-puff from the Works.

'It goes on, goes on,' said Harriet, her head against the cork tree. 'I wonder what is going to happen to us?' And by that she meant, of course, 'What is going to happen to me?'

There were ways of telling. Nan used sometimes to play charms with them. She dropped pieces of lead tinfoil into a saucepan of boiling water, and, when they were softened, she lifted them out with a spoon on to a cold plate where they hardened. Whatever shapes they made told your future.

They played this one Sunday morning some three weeks after Diwali when Valerie had come to spend the day. Captain John, too, had limped up the drive after breakfast, and was there, sitting by Nan, his stick propped by his chair.

He is always here, always, thought Harriet crossly. And so is Valerie. Why should they be? Haven't they homes of their own?

She noticed now that, when Captain John was alone with them, some of the stiffness went out of his face. Sometimes he laughed and his eyes were not unlike Bogey's, except that Bogey's were quick and his had often a curious emptiness; but they were gentle too. Yes, he has nice eyes, Harriet admitted, but I wish he were not so jerky. 'Why is he so jerky?' she had asked Mother irritably. 'Because he was hurt so badly,' said Mother. 'Unbearably hurt.'

Looking at Captain John now in the light of this soft warm morning, as he bent his head down by Victoria's, as Victoria leant against his knee, it was difficult to think of him as being unbearably hurt. Unbearably? questioned Harriet, wrinkling her forehead. What is unbearable? When I caught my nail in the railway carriage door I went mad with pain. Mad. Then why isn't he mad? Why didn't he die? What is it that made him live and not go mad? 'He must be stronger than we think,' said Harriet, looking at Captain John.

She considered him, as he put Victoria carefully away and took the saucepan from Nan, to let Nan have a change and rest. His hands were steady now, and his face had colour from the warmth of the fire. He looked big, yes, almost strong among the children, and his hair, that was dark, patched with white, was attractive. Like a magpie, thought Harriet. Why, he is very good-looking, thought Harriet in surprise.

She knew Nan admired him. 'He is like a young prince,' said Nan.

'A funny kind of a prince!' Harriet had said. 'And he isn't young, Nan.'

'He is, poor boy.'

'Oh Nan!' said Harriet impatiently. 'And why does he come all the time – all the time?'

'Perhaps – we have something he needs,' said Nan.

'What?'

'I don't know. We must pray for him. He will go on when he is ready,' said Nan.

'Go on? Where?' asked Harriet, but Nan did not say. Instead, she added in her admonitory seeing-through-Harriet voice, 'Now you are not to go saying anything to him, Harriet.'

'As if I would,' said Harriet indignantly, but she knew that Nan was right and that probably her curiosity would get the better of her. A young prince, thought Harriet now. She was not quite so sure that Nan was wrong.

'Captain John,' said Valerie, 'will you drop a charm for me?' Valerie, by courtesy of the family to her place as visitor, had been given the first turn. Why then should she have another so soon?

'It is Harriet's turn,' said Captain John crisply, and Harriet heard him, and she knew, warmly, in an instant as she heard this crispness in his voice, that he did not like Valerie either, and did not approve of her. Harriet came closer.

The smell of live charcoal from the brazier filled the verandah with the smell of hot lead from the charms and the smell of warmth in the starch of Nan's apron. Ram Prasad, who was always with the children in all their games, blew up the fire as Captain John dropped a charm for Harriet. The lead melted, ran wide, and he caught it in the spoon and lifted it and dropped it again on the plate, but curiously, the pellet ran together, sizzling, again, and formed itself into a round ball.

'It is round,' said Bogey, 'like a marble.'

'It is a world,' said Victoria. They did not understand her until Nan reminded them of the globe of the world on Father's desk.

'It *is* a world,' said Harriet, taking it in her hand now it had cooled. On its rough surface she imagined she saw seas and lands. 'I wonder what it means?'

'Well, Harriet, are you satisfied? Now you have the whole world?' said Valerie.

Harriet gave her a long straight look.

'It is your turn, Captain John,' she said, wanting to reciprocate. 'Let us make a charm for you. Let us see what you are going to be.'

Valerie nudged her sharply. 'What a silly you are!' she whispered down Harriet's neck. 'You will make him feel awful. How can *he* be anything?'

But – he has to be, thought Harriet. Of course he has to be. He didn't die.

'What do you want to be?' asked the little Victoria, putting her head back to look at him. 'What could you be?'

There was a long silence. No one had any suggestion to make. 'Oh well,' said Victoria, 'I think you had better just stay here with us.'

'Make a charm for Bea,' said Nan.

Bea had a loop, a circle, that made a rough little ring. 'That means you will be loved and married,' said Nan.

Bea took the ring and looked at it by the verandah rail, turning it over and over in her fingers. After Captain John gave the saucepan back to Nan, he stood up and stretched, and limped over to Bea.

'What is the name of those flowers?' he asked Bea, presently.

'Poinsettias,' said Bea, politely.

'They make me realize I am in India,' said Captain John. 'They look so hot and red, even in the rain. And those, those little low pale blue ones on the bushes?'

'Plumbago,' said Bea.

'This is a lovely garden,' he said.

Why, thought Harriet, does he talk to Bea so – earnestly? He was not talking to Bea as if she were a child, but as if she were grown-up. Bea is a little girl, thought Harriet, and why is Bea so polite? There is no need to be so polite to him.

'I am glad you like it,' said Bea.

'I think it is the most beautiful garden I have ever seen,' said Captain John, earnestly.

It was a beautiful garden. The poinsettias grew round the plinth of the house, huge scarlet-fingered flowers with milk sap in their stems: The house was large, square, of grey stucco, with verandahs along its double floors and tiers of great green-shuttered windows. It had a flat roof, with a parapet where the children played, and the parapet was carved with huge stone daisies. Can a house, a serious house, be carved with daisies? This was.

Below the poinsettias was the plumbago; it made hedges of nursery pale blue and the flowerbeds it bordered would later be full of the pansies and verbena and mignonette that were now in seed pans in a seed-table made of bamboo. Along the paths were ranged pots of violets that held the dew. Other pots of chrysanthemums were on the verandah and in a double phalanx down the steps. These chrysanthemums had mammoth heads of flowers that were white and yellow and bronze and pink; some of them were larger than the children's heads. Later, in their place, there would be potted petunias.

The lawns rolled away to the river under the trees, but there were flowers, bougainvillaeas, that spread themselves into clumps and up the trees, orange, purple, magenta and cerise, like Bea's hair ribbon; there were Marechal-Neil turrets with their small lemon-yellow roses, and other roses in the rose garden, and bushes of the small white Bengali roses tinged with pink. There were standard hibiscus that were out already in pinks, and creams and yellows and reds, and morning glory and other creepers, on the house, over the porch, along screens, up trees: jasmine and orange-keyed begonias, passion flowers and quisqualis that would flower in January and the spring; now there was only the pink-and-white sandwich creeper out and Bea's bridal creeper over the gate. There were squirrels and lizards in the garden and birds: bulbuls and kingfishers and doves and the magpie robin and sunbirds and tree pies and wagtails and hawks. Birds are little live landmarks and more truthful than flowers; they cannot be transplanted, nor grafted, nor turned blue and pink. The birds were in the flavour of that garden, as the white paddy birds and the vultures were part of the flavour of the fields, and the circling kites and the kingfishers of the river; the garden was full of swallowtail butterflies bigger than the sunbirds and of Bogey's insects and Bogey's ants; no one really knew the insects except Bogey. At night there were sometimes jackals on the lawn and fireflies, and there was a bush that used to fill the whole house with its scent in the darkness, a bush called Lady-of-the-Night.

Harriet's cork tree stood on the edge of the drive, directly in front of the steps. It was as high as the house. Soon it would bud, then be covered in blossom, and the flowers, when they fell at the end of the winter, would make a circle deep in flowers on the grass. Woodpeckers lived in the cork tree and in season it had Japanese lilies round its foot.

Now Captain John was looking at it. 'And that is a most beautiful tree,' he said.

'It is Harriet's,' Bea told him.

'Harriet's?' He said it as if he were surprised, and Harriet was suddenly oddly shy, and oddly pleased.

'At least, she says it is hers, though I don't know why,' said Bea.

Harriet felt his look bent on herself for a moment, but when she brought herself to look up, she saw that he had forgotten her; he was looking down at Bea and she had a sudden remembrance of him on Diwali night. She had felt him looking at something then, or someone, and she had followed his look and found it on Bea. Why? Why did he look at Bea? Now he was looking at Bea again with that same extreme gentleness and interest. Then Bea, too, looked up and back at him.

'Let me see your ring,' he said.

Bea gave him a curiously startled glance and dropped the ring into his hand from above and walked away to the others.

Nan had made a charm for Victoria. It was scoop shape.

'It is a bucket,' said Victoria.

'Or a thimble,' said Nan.

Nan and Victoria could not have appeared more different. Victoria was very plump, very blonde, built into a beautiful heavy pink and pearl fleshed body with dimples at the joints and fat bracelets at the joins; especially inviting were the backs of her legs and thighs. She shone by contrast with Nan, the old Anglo-Indian, who was thin, small, very dark, with a fine brown skin that was slack and tired now and showed bluish shadows and pouches under her eyes. Her hands were small and thin and busy, and her fingers were wrinkled and pricked at the tips with a lifetime of washing and sewing. Her hair was black and dry and thin and held, each side of her head, by tortoiseshell combs. She wore a striped dress and an apron that had a convent thinness and cleanness. Her eyes were like Victoria's, brown and clear; as her body receded it seemed to leave all her life in her eyes.

Besides their eyes, Nan and Victoria were alike in that, at the moment, they were both perfect. Victoria had reached the stage of completed babyhood; little girls, especially, sometimes linger in this stage for three or four months, and during that time they are quite unconsciously perfect. Victoria had no troubles, she did not trouble anyone, and nor did Nan. Nan had completed her hard womanhood, and she had managed to shed her troubles. She had reclaimed, through living and service, what Victoria had not yet lost.

Then Nan made Bogey's charm.

Sometimes the charms did not act, and now Bogey's refused to coagulate. It ran and spread on the plate and took no shape at all.

'What is the matter with it?' said Harriet. 'How can we tell what it means?'

'It won't tell,' said Nan.

'Put it back and try again, Nan.'

'No,' said Nan. 'If it won't tell, it won't. I am sorry, Bogey.'

'I don't mind,' said Bogey, cheerfully. He picked up the still soft lead and rolled it into a ball like Harriet's and began to play marbles with it.

Harriet left the others and went away. It was Valerie's turn for another charm and she did not want to see Valerie's turn. She went on to the drive and under the cork tree, and looked up at it, thinking of how Captain John had admired it. She herself did not think it was as beautiful as the jacaranda trees, for instance, or even as the peepul tree in the wall by Ram Prasad's house that stood at the gate. 'But I like it,' said Harriet aloud.

She saw a crevice in the trunk low enough for her to

reach. Stepping over the lilies, she fitted her charm neatly into it, and the ball rolled down and lay in the five-inch hollow at the bottom. She could reach it with her fingers, but she left it there. That is a safe place, thought Harriet. Now I can find it again. Bogey might play marbles with his charm, but she was sure that hers was an omen.

Each year there were nests in the garden. There was always a sunbird's nest in the bougainvillaea that grew up the house wall; a long untidy tear-shaped nest made of fibres and dried leaves with the sunbirds shimmering in and out. Now there was a dove's nest in the creeper above the verandah; you could see her sitting on her nest; she would sit there quiet for hours; her breast was grey, flecked with brown.

'What is she doing?' asked Victoria.

'Brooding,' said Captain John. He spoke often, and very kindly, to Victoria.

He was staying in the house. Mother had made him come over from the Red House so that she and Nan could look after him, because the wound in his good leg had opened and was discharging.

'It can't be very good then,' said Harriet.

'It isn't, but it is the best I have,' said Captain John.

'He shouldn't work here, in this climate,' Harriet heard Father say. 'It is cruelty,' but Captain John managed to work, though he looked ill and frayed and stiff and worn, and he managed to speak kindly to Victoria, though he did lose his temper with the rest of them.

'Brooding?' said Victoria, looking up at the nest. 'Is that brooding?' she said. 'She looks ... happy.'

'I think she is,' said Captain John, seriously. 'She sits on her nest and she feels the whole world going round her, and she takes everything she wants from the world and puts it into her eggs.'

'You shouldn't tell Victoria things like that,' said Bea. 'She thinks they are true.'

'But they are true,' said Captain John.

'How queer you are,' said Bea. 'You say such queer things,' and Captain John's thin cheek suddenly burnt and he put up his hand to smooth his hair, which was a trick he had to hide his stiffness. His hand was shaking again. Why does he *mind* Bea? thought Harriet. She knew, then, that it was too tiring for him to speak as he wanted to do, to Bea. It was much more restful for him to bark, as he barked to Harriet, 'Blast you, Harry. Take your great hand off my leg. You hurt me.' He would never say that to Bea. 'And he isn't queer,' said Harriet. 'That about the dove was nice.'

'Are we in eggs?' asked Victoria.

'You are,' said Harriet, teasing her. 'Father says you are still in the egg, Victoria.'

It was funny to think that she, Harriet, who was still a child herself, could remember a time when Victoria, standing so large and solid on the verandah beside them, was not. Then there was no Victoria. And there was no gap before, thought Harriet, puzzled. There was no empty place and yet we fitted her in. It was funny, and notable, that families always did fit the babies in. Then she remembered, what she was supposed to know and had been told and still could not yet realize, that soon, in a month or two, or three or was it four, they, the family, were to have another baby themselves.

'Did you know that?' she asked Captain John.

'Know what?'

'How do you expect people to understand what you are talking of, if you go thinking in between?' said Valerie. Bea did not defend Harriet, but looked at her severely too.

Harriet left them.

'Are we in eggs?' Victoria had asked. Fancy asking that,

thought Harriet, wandering away, but it would be funny if we were. As she said it, she was frightened. She had too often this feeling of being enclosed, shut in a small shape like a dome, and, if it were an egg, she had no beak to break it. 'How can I get out? I never can get out,' she was just going to say in a panic, and then she remembered that, if she were in an egg, just like the chick, she would grow too big for it and break it. The thing is to grow very quickly, said Harriet to herself, and she said aloud, 'Nan says we change our skin seven times in our lives. Perhaps this is the same idea.'

'That is snakes, not people,' said Bogey. 'Harry, Ram Prasad says there is a cobra under the peepul tree, but you are not to tell. We are going to watch it. Perhaps we shall see it change its skin,' said Bogey.

'Ugh!' said Harriet. She had none of Bogey's freemasonry with insects and reptiles, but in fascinated horror she went with him to the peepul tree. The garden wall was built each side, into its trunk, so that it formed part of the wall and half of it was in the garden and half in the road outside. Harriet knew why the cobra, if there were a cobra, had come there. It was because the front part of the tree in the road was a shrine with a whitewashed plinth and the villagers used to put saucers of milk on it with offerings of rice and burnt sugar and curd. Snakes like milk, and Harriet guessed it had come there for that.

She and Bogey squatted on their heels, watching the roots, but nothing stirred. At any moment Harriet expected the horrid bronze-grey lengths of the snake to come flowing out, over, and under, the roots. 'Ugh!' shuddered Harriet, and when at last she tired and stood up, her hands and the backs of her knees where she had folded them were wet. 'I don't want to see it,' she said. 'Bogey. You know I am sure we ought to tell. We are supposed to tell if we see a snake in the garden.'

Bogey had not heard. He was still squatting, still waiting, the whole of him intent on the snake hole. It was not that Bogey was disobedient as much as blithely unaware he had been told. 'Oh well,' said Harriet, 'we haven't seen it yet, and it isn't really in the garden. It is in the peepul tree.'

She went back to the house, and on her way she passed Victoria with her doll. 'I play so beautifully with my baby,' she said to Harriet as Harriet passed. 'She was born again yesterday.'

'You are always having her born,' said Harriet scornfully.

'Why not?' asked Victoria. 'You can be born again and again, can't you?'

It was puzzling. Every time Harriet examined somebody's silly remark, it seemed not to be so silly. 'I don't understand it,' she said, and she wondered who could explain it to her; its surface silliness was such that she doubted if she would find anyone to whom she could make clear what she wanted to ask. Then she made up her mind; she would risk a chance and ask Captain John.

He may swear at me, thought Harriet. He likes Bea, but never mind, he can talk to me for once, thought Harriet. If he laughs at me, he laughs at me. Never mind. And she wavered no more, but went to look for him.

He was leaning on the verandah rail, idling, looking at the sun and the flowers, quiet and dreaming.

'Captain John,' said Harriet, interrupting him, 'I want to talk to you.'

'Must you?' he said lazily.

'Yes, I must; about being born.'

He still did not seem willing. 'Can't you talk to Bea or Nan about that, Harriet? I can't talk about being born.'

'Oh, but you can,' said Harriet, putting a compelling hand on him. 'I don't want to be told anything. I want to talk.'

He looked down at her, his face lazy, not at all stiff.

'Do you know, your eyes have speckles in them, flecks?' he said.

'Like the dove's breast?' asked Harriet.

He looked at her more particularly. 'What dove?'

'The dove on her nest. I liked that – what you said.'

'Did you?' he said, and he seemed pleased. Talking to Harriet he had not changed his lounging, dreaming attitude, and he forgot to smooth his hair and pull his tie straight. He looked down into her eyes lazily without thinking of himself.

'Listen,' said Harriet, and leaning on the rail beside him, she told him of what she was thinking, puzzling over, and it came in words that were unusually clear, almost crystalline. She told him of Victoria's remark and of how it was silly and yet it rang true; of his own remark that Bea said was queer and yet was true too. 'Is everything a bit true then?' asked Harriet.

She could see the peepul tree over the bamboo clumps that hid its lower half, and she wondered idly if the cobra had come out. 'Ugh!' said Harriet again, and moved her shoulders in a shudder while she waited for Captain John to speak.

'My idea,' said Captain John, 'isn't very different from

Victoria's, though she didn't mean hers in this way. I have an idea,' said Captain John, his eyes looking now, not at Harriet, but across the rail to the garden, 'that we go on being born again and again because we have to, with each thing that happens to us, each new episode.'

'What is an episode?'

'It really means an incident ... between two acts.'

'I don't understand.'

'Call it an incident, a happening. With each new happening, perhaps with each person we meet if they are important to us, we must either be born again, or die a little bit; big deaths and little ones, big and little births.'

'I should think it would be better to go on being born, than to die all the time,' said Harriet.

'If we can,' said Captain John, 'but it takes a bit of doing. It is called growing, Harriet, and it is often painful and difficult. On the whole, it is very much easier to die.'

'But you didn't,' said Harriet.

'I just managed not to, but I am no criterion,' said Captain John.

'What is a criterion?' asked Harriet, and before he could answer, she asked, 'Who is it who is important to you, Captain John?'

'Never you mind,' and he stood up and stretched himself. 'Do you think you could leave me alone now like a good girl?'

Harriet went along to the jetty and sat down in her usual place. 'I *wish* he had told me,' she said. She hung her feet down above the water; they were still bare, and she had still, so far, not had hookworm. Wriggling her toes to feel the dust between them, she wondered, all at once, how she, Harriet, appeared to Captain John. Then she wondered, more truthfully, if he ever saw her at all. 'But he said that about my eyes,' argued Harriet. 'Yes, he said they had flecks in them,' but if that were in derision or admiration she did not know. She thought again of the way she had seen him looking at Bea when they lit the lamps for Diwali. They had been on the roof, in the darkness, and the point of light from each lamp lit a circle round itself but was not strong enough to lighten the whole roof darkness. Anyone bending over a lamp was suddenly illumined and Bea, bending to shift the oil round a wick, was lit, her shoulders, her neck, the line of her face, and her hair; she was gilded, and as she moved the oil she looked up at Valerie and laughed at what Valerie was saying. Harriet had noticed that Captain John had stood there, lost, and the oil in the lamp he held ran over the edge on to the floor and Valerie scolded him. 'Yes, he looks at Bea,' said Harriet mournfully.

She wished her big toe could reach the water. The river current gurgled against the poles of the jetty; its traffic floated down and Harriet watched it lazily, while her mind left that part of Captain John's idea and thought of the other. *You are born with each new big thing that happens.* I don't quite understand that, thought Harriet.

A boat floated down laden with bright red pots: then a boat laden with nothing at all; then a launch from up-river; Harriet noted its black funnel, blue-banded, and its white and red hull: From Brentford's, she thought, the 'Sprite'. On its deck sat a large lady dressed in white. Mrs Milligan, Harriet identified her without a flicker of interest. How few, how very, very few people are important, she thought, and lazily she began to think over the people who were important for her. Father-Mother-Bea-Bogey-Victoria. That was automatic, and she did not realize that, as she said their names, she did not think of them at all. Nan? Her hesitation made her think of Nan. No, not Nan, thought Harriet as she watched a police motor boat, with the police flag almost touching the wash at its stern as it went by; the rolling wave behind it presently came in broken rifts to hit the jetty where she was sitting. Anyone else? thought Harriet. Of course, children were not expected to have many people, but however she circumscribed herself, her thoughts came back to the question she wanted to ask. Captain John? asked Harriet at last, and she answered as she had to answer because it was the truth, How can he be important for me? It is Bea he likes. At first we thought it was Victoria, but it is Bea he is interested in.

A porpoise came down, turning slowly over and over in midstream with a beautiful easy armchair rhythmical motion that lulled Harriet. She rubbed her back against the post and picked at her finger lump with her hand. Oh well, thought Harriet comfortably, I shall meet heaps of people when I am older, when I am famous. Heaps of things are going to happen to me.

A whirr and a splash made her jump so that she almost fell off the jetty. A kingfisher had struck from a branch above her. Now it sat on a post with the fish still bending and jerking in its beak. The poor fish had been placidly, happily, swimming and feeding somewhere under the jetty, and then, out of its element, from another, it had been seized and carried off. And swallowed, thought Harriet regretfully, watching it disappear.

I wonder what the other fishes think? thought Harriet, but then, that was the same with any dying; one person was seized and taken away. But what does it feel like if that comes right plumb in the middle of your family? She could not think of it, it seemed impossible and yet she had just seen it happen. Things do happen, she told herself, but she was lulled again with the sound of the river running in her ears. Those were fishes, Harriet told herself comfortably. Only fishes.

There was no sign of the splash. The river ran steadily where it had been. 'There you see ... Anything can happen, anything, and whatever happens the other fishes just go on wriggling and swimming and feeding because they have to,' said Harriet. 'It, the river, has to go on.' Whatever happened, a fish's death, a wreck, storm, sun, the river assimilated it all. The far bank showed as a line across the river, a line of fields, a clump of trees by the temple, and, further away, the walls and roofs and chimney and jetty of Valerie's father's works. I wonder what he thinks about dying; Captain John, not Valerie's father, thought Harriet idly. I wonder if he thinks the same as he thinks about being born, if he really thinks you could die over and over again. Goodness, thought Harriet, I nearly died just now when I nearly fell off the jetty. I would die if I saw that cobra! But what Captain John meant was deeper than that. Harriet suspected that, but her mind was now too lazy, too happy, to explore.

Sometimes, in the night, Harriet thought about death. She thought about Father and Mother dying, or Nan, who was really very old; then she would hastily wake Bea to comfort her.

When Ram Prasad's wife died, she was carried on a string bed to the river and put on a pyre and burned. Afterwards her ashes were thrown on the water. Bogey and Harriet went to look, though they knew without being told that Mother would not have allowed them.

'Did you mind it?' Harriet asked Bogey afterwards.

'Mind what?'

'The burning.'

'It looked just like burning to me.'

It had. The pyre was well alight when they arrived, hiding themselves behind a brick kiln on the edge of the burning ghat so that even Ram Prasad should not see them.

'I didn't like the smell,' said Harriet. 'Did you see them throw her ashes in the river?'

'I wasn't looking,' said Bogey, 'there was a frog . . .' His mind went off on the thought of the frog, but after a while he said, 'No, I didn't mind.'

'Nor did I,' said Harriet. She had not seen the body, only those ashes, and they did not seem to be anything to do with a person who had lived and walked and talked and eaten food and played with her baby and laughed. No, it had been, up to now, birds like the kingfisher, and animals like the livestock of the nursery, guinea-pigs and rabbits and kittens, that had given Harriet her glimpses of birth and death.

Nan said if you were good you died and went to heaven. 'To Paradise.' Mother, not so certainly, half-heartedly, lent some support to that. Nan was quite certain.

'To eternal rest,' said Nan, looking at the swellings her bunions made in her shoes. 'To have wings like the angels,' said Nan, as she toiled upstairs with the washing.

Harriet had seen heaven on the films, but it was a Hindu heaven in an Indian film, Krishna playing his flute in a garden of roses and dancing girls. The Mohammedan heaven? She was not sure about that. She asked Father what Buddhists did when they died; he took down a book and read to her about a drop sliding into the crystal sea and being lost. She asked Mother, and Mother pointed out that Harriet knew already that Jesus rose from the dead; some people, she added, believed that you came back over and over again, to live another life each time. 'A better life,' said Mother.

'Goodness, how good you must be in the end,' said Harriet.

That was the idea, Mother thought, and if you were not good, she went on to say, you came back as something lower.

'Like?'

'An animal. An insect. A flea,' said Mother, smiling.

I should rather like to be a flea, thought Harriet, thinking of herself as a gay acrobatic jumping flea, but Bogey, who did not like to be labelled good or bad, was bored with the idea. 'I should rather have done with it,' said Bogey.

All these thoughts seemed like cracks in the wholeness of Harriet's unconsciousness. It had cracked before, of course, but now she was growing rapaciously.

The winter drew on. Day succeeded day, and ended and went out of sight and was gone. There are such lots of days, thought Harriet, but not more than there are drops of water in the river.

She was on the jetty again. Very often now she went

to watch the river. It flowed down in negroid peace, in sun, in green strong water. Harriet, now she was growing from a little girl into a big one, was beginning to sense its peace. 'It comes from a source,' said Harriet, who learnt geography. 'From very far away, from a trickle from a spring, no one knows where exactly, or perhaps they do know; it doesn't matter. It is going to something far bigger than itself, though it, itself, looks big enough. It is going to the sea,' said Harriet, 'and nothing will stop it. Nothing stops days, or rivers,' said Harriet with certainty.

Then the guinea-pig, Bathsheba, died.

The children had several scores of guinea-pigs and they used to play shepherds with them, driving guinea-pig flocks over the lawn. One of the original stock was Bathsheba, an old white guinea-pig, who belonged to Harriet. One day, Harriet found her, lying limp, as if she were asleep, in a corner of the cage. When Harriet picked her up, she did not feel limp, but curiously stiff and resilient and her fur felt hard. 'She is dead, I think,' said Harriet, but she was still not quite sure what dead was. She did not take Bathsheba into Nan or Mother or anyone in the house; she carried her down the garden and out of the gate and into the Red

House to find Captain John, but all the assistants were out except one, Mr Corsie, lying ill in bed with dysentery.

'May I come in, Mr Corsie?' asked Harriet.

'Wh't is it ye want?' asked Mr Corsie without enthusiasm. He was feeling ill.

'Please – is this dead?' asked Harriet, offering Bathsheba for inspection.

'Ugh! Take it away, oot o'heer,' cried Mr Corsie.

'*Is* it – ugh?' asked Harriet, doubtfully.

'Dae ye no heer me?' asked Mr Corsie. 'Take it oot. Or I'll tell yeer Pa.'

'But – is it dead?' asked Harriet.

'Daid as a doornail. Take it away. Good Lorrd! It is stinkin'.'

Harriet immediately dropped Bathsheba on the floor.

That night she was worried.

'Bea.'

'Sssh.'

'Bea.'

'What *is* it, Harriet? I am asleep.'

'Bea, when we are dead, do we go . . . like Bathsheba?'

'How did she go?' asked Bea, yawning.

'Stiff. Hard. Stinking,' said Harriet tearfully.

'Yes, I suppose we do,' said Bea, who was sleepy. 'That is called a corpse.'

Harriet shivered, all over her skin, under the bedclothes.

'Bea.'

Silence.

'Bea.'

No answer.

'Bea. *Bea. BEA!*'

'Oh, Harriet! I am asleep, What is it?'

'Bea. I don't want to.'

'Don't want to *what?*'

'Be a corpse.'

'But you are not,' said Bea, practically.

'But I shall be,' said Harriet, and she began to cry.

'Don't you think you could wait till you are,' said Bea. 'I *am* so sleepy, Harriet.' Then as the fact of Harriet's sobs was borne in upon her, she said, more gently, 'Couldn't you wait till the morning, Harry?'

'No. No. I can't,' sobbed Harriet. 'I am frightened, Bea. I can't get the feeling of Bathsheba off my hands. I am frightened, Bea.'

'Don't cry,' said Bea, kindly. She sat up in bed, and by the verandah light Harriet could see her shoulders in her white yoked nightgown, and the fall of her dark hair.

'Don't cry, Harry. It isn't anything to cry about. I am sure it is not.'

The sound of her normal little voice was comforting to Harriet, until she thought that Bea too must die, dark hair, voice and all. 'Then I shall never hear her voice again,' cried Harriet silently, 'and Mother must die, and Nan, and Nan is old and must die quite soon.'

'Why isn't it something to cry about?' cried Harriet bitterly, aloud.

'Oh, Harry. You ask too many questions.'

'Yes, but ... Don't *you* ever think about dying, Bea?'

'Well, yes I do,' said Bea.

'Then what do you think?' she asked.

'It is hard to know what I think,' said Bea's small voice out of the darkness. 'But I know a few things.'

'Wh-what do you know?' quavered Harriet, and she said suspiciously, 'Nan and Mother and Ram Prasad tell us things about heaven and Jesus and Bhramo, but they don't really know.'

'I think they are all wrong,' said Bea severely. 'Mine are not things like that. They are more simple things.' And she added, as if this had only just occurred to her, 'More sensible things.'

'Wh-what sort of th-things?'

'This,' said Bea. 'When anything, anybody, is dead, like Bathsheba, it is dead. The life, the breath, the ... the *warm* in it, is gone.'

'Nan calls it the spirit.'

'The spirit then,' said Bea. 'I call it the "warm", but the spirit or the warm is gone.'

'Yes,' said Harriet. 'Yes. It was gone out of Bathsheba.'

'The body is left behind,' said Bea, 'and what happens to it? It goes bad.'

'Don't!' said Harriet, and shuddered.

'You can't keep a body ...'

'Except mummies and those Rajahs who are pickled in honey,' said Harriet.

'Then I think,' said Bea, and she contradicted herself. 'Then I *know* that it isn't meant to go on. It is useless. The body isn't any use any more.'

'Yes?' said Harriet.

'But the other, the warm, has gone. It doesn't stay and go bad. So I think,' said Bea, 'that it is of some use. That it has gone to something, somewhere.'

'But where?' asked Harriet. 'Where?'

'You ask too many questions, Harry,' said Bea.

'I wonder what Captain John thinks,' said Harriet in despair.

'Captain *John?*'

'Yes. He would think something,' said Harriet, and her curiosity got the better of her sense, and she said, 'What do you feel like with Captain John, Bea?'

Bea immediately lay down again. Harriet knew she would not tell.

But, as silence settled, Harriet felt obscurely comforted. Why? Bea had not said much, but Harriet felt strengthened. She kept her head under the bedclothes for a little while and then found she was perfectly well able to come out, and she lay calmly, looking through her mosquito net at the starlight that fell dimly between the columns of the verandah, and listening to the puff-wait-puff of steam from the works and the ever-flowing gurgling of the river. I will learn more about it as I grow, she thought comfortably. Living and dying and being born, like Captain John said, she yawned. She naturally supposed that that growing was still a great way off.

She tried to remember the names of the stars as she lay, and she thought how much longer stars and things like trees and rocks went on than people: Mountains and islands and sands, she thought, and man-made things as well; songs and pictures and rare vases and poems. 'Things are the thing,' said Harriet sleepily, and then a thought came like a spear from one of those stars, but real, truthful. It had occurred to her that she, Harriet, might possibly, one day, if she were good enough, have some small part in that. One of my poems might still be alive in, thought Harriet, say, AD 4000. It might. I don't say it will, but it might. I should be like the Chinese poets, she thought dizzily. Or like Keats or Shakespeare, she thought, and she was filled with a sense of her own responsibility. That was a new sensation for Harriet. She was not given to responsibility and it gave her a feeling, more serious, more humble, than she had ever known. 'I must work,' said Harriet earnestly. 'I must work and work and work.' Like Queen Victoria, she thought. I will be good. I will be good.

Saw roses wide that comforted her heart

And saw their cr-im-son ... but it was somehow not interesting. She gave a huge yawn, the poem grew fuddled, and she was asleep.

Next morning, when she went out before breakfast and stood on the jetty, she wondered what all the fuss had been about. Now she felt she had no need to stand there staring at the river, watching it flow, when it was such a glorious morning in the garden. 'What was I fussing about last night?' she asked. She was filled with such buoyancy of living, of happiness, that she could not stay still any longer; she had to move away, walking up and down the paths, beside the creeper screens, under the turrets of roses, touching the flowers, knocking the dew off them, letting the boughs touch her and spring back, until she came to the cork tree.

It was early. The garden shone. The cold weather light lay on the paths and unfolded across the green of the lawns and through the trees. There was brighter green in the wings of the flycatchers and in the flight of parakeets that flew in front of her and across the river.

Victoria came down the steps. She did not see Harriet. She had some straw under her arm and she was dragging a rug after her. Harriet knew what she was going to do; she was going to make a house. At the moment Victoria was like a snail, she always had a house attached to her somewhere. Now, dragging the rug over the dew and the gravel, she went away round the corner towards the swing.

Harriet had reached the cork tree. By standing very quietly under it, she could hear the woodpeckers tap-tapping on it far above her head. She put her head back and looked through the break in the branches and their canopy to the sky, and as she looked, the clouds, and the grey line with a stone daisy that was the parapet of the house, and the tall tree itself, seemed to tilt gently backwards. That is the world turning, thought Harriet. It gave her a large feeling to see the tilt of the world. Clouds, house, tree, lawns, river, Harriet, were borne slowly backwards as the world turned, but the tree remained upright, steady, rising into the sky, spreading its branches that were coming into bud. Under Harriet's feet, where she stood among the red lilies, its roots went deep into the earth, down down into the pit of the earth. 'I believe,' said Harriet, 'I believe that this is the middle of the world. That I am standing in the middle of the middle of the world, and this tree is that tree, the axis tree, like the one in the story. It goes right through the earth. It goes up and up.'

She put her hand on the tree and she thought she was drawn up into its height as if she were soaring out of the earth. Her ears seemed to sing. She had the feeling of soaring, then she came back to stand at the foot of the tree, her hand on the bark, and she began to write a new poem in her head.

It took her a long time, walking on the lawn, pacing the paths, coming back to the tree, to finish it. She finished it in her head, then she felt for her book that was in the waistband of her dress, and her pencil that she kept in her stocking, and wrote the poem down.

When she looked at it, it did not look like any of her poems. She read it aloud. It did not sound like any of her poems. 'It is not like any poem I ever read,' she said doubtfully. 'It can't be good,' and immediately she had the feeling that it was good. It felt alive, as she did. She felt alive and curiously powerful, and full of what seemed to her a glory.

She glanced round. She could see Victoria's head rising and dipping by the swing, but it was no good reading poems to Victoria. Bea was out riding, she did not know where Bogey was, and every adult was always busy before breakfast. Then, as she stood puzzled under the cork tree, Captain John came limping up the jetty and across the lawn towards her.

'Hallo,' said Captain John.

'Hallo,' said Harriet, considering him.

'I have been across the river.'

'Bea has gone riding,' said Harriet. She looked up at him. 'Captain John,' she said, and stopped.

'Yes?'

'I—' said Harriet slowly, and then easily it tumbled

out. 'I have written a poem. It is – either very bad – I expect it is bad, or else it is good. It is so new, I don't know.'

'Show me,' said Captain John, and put out his hand. Harriet gave him the poem and he began to read it.

She had not expected he would read it aloud, quite naturally and unselfconsciously as he was doing, and prickings of acute shyness ran over her until she found that she was soothed, allayed, delighted by the sound of her own words:

'This tree, my tree, is the pole of the world . . .'

When he had finished it he looked at Harriet. Then he looked at the poem.

'Did *you* write this?' he asked. 'By yourself?'

Harriet nodded. She could not speak.

'Nobody helped you?'

'Of course not,' said Harriet indignantly.

'But it is good!'

Waves of bright-eyed satisfaction chased through Harriet's every vein. He looked at her as if he had not properly seen her before.

'It – felt good . . . for me,' said Harriet huskily.

'I didn't know you wrote poems.'

'I – I do,' said Harriet. She had to bend her head down.

She moved the toe of her shoe along the edge of a root.
The silence went on and on. She could hear the woodpeckers again, tap, tap, tap.

'Har-ree!'

That was Bogey.

'Har-ree!' She raised her head.

'He-ah!'

Bogey came chasing round the corner of the house,
past Victoria, past the swing.

'Here, Boge. I am here.'

'We are going to make bricks,' announced Bogey, ''n
bake them in a n'oven, 'n build a tank for fishes. I have
found some lovely mud. It is a little bit smelly, but you
needn't mind. Come on, Harry.'

The gate opened and Bea came trotting up the drive
on the white pony, Pearl. Bogey ran off and Harriet sped
after him.

But when she reached the corner of the house she
stopped and turned so fast that the short skirt of her dress
whirled round her. She stood in the shadow of the poinsettias and looked back at Bea and Captain John. She saw
how Captain John went up and put his hand on the
pony's neck and then how Bea let him help her off as if
she were a grown-up, not a child. Harriet stood, frowning

a little by the poinsettias, then slowly she walked away to look at Bogey's mud.

Now Harriet began to think a great deal about Captain John.

What was wrong with him? Something was wrong. There was that emptiness in his eyes. Though he was loosed, among people again, he was not like other people, and he knew it. 'But he was strong enough not to die,' argued Harriet. He was strong enough to bear the unbearable pain, and the prison camp, and to escape, and to live in the hospital through all those operations when no one expected him to live, and to go on working every day with his troublesome wound and the weight of his leg. He could joke about it; he could be kind to Victoria, and in the same way to Nan; he could understand her, Harriet: he had this . . . 'this reverent,' said Harriet, wrinkling her brow to get the exact word, 'this reverent feeling for Bea'; and even someone as young as Harriet could sense he was no common thinker. There was no one she could talk to like Captain John. 'And he *ought* to talk to me,' said Harriet. 'When he talks to me he looks quite strong and rested. He doesn't when he talks to Bea.'

'You can't talk to her, can you?' she asked him.

'No,' he said irritably. 'She is too confoundedly polite.'
That was the first time Harriet had ever heard a word
against politeness, but she saw immediately that it was
true.

But it was not Bea who was wrong with Captain John.
It was something in him, himself. 'Or not in him,' she
said slowly.

'Leave him alone,' said Nan.

'But I want to *do* something for him.'

'You can pray for him.'

'Oh *Nan*!'

'You can,' said Nan certainly, and then she added, as a
warning, 'and, Harriet, you are not to do anything else.'

But Harriet, being Harriet, did, and was snubbed.

She went away with his snub stinging in her, into the
Secret Hole, where she sat down on her box, in the dark-
est shade. She sat holding her knees in her arms, her face
turned down on them, and the stinging passed into a
peculiar hurt. 'I – I hate him,' said Harriet, with clenched
teeth.

Ayah came presently and found her. 'What is it, Harry
Baba? What is it, Harriet Rajah?'

'I have a pain,' said Harriet, she did not know what
else to call it.

Ayah began to rub her legs, though the pain, of course, was not in her legs. Harriet had had pains in her legs and arms recently that Nan called 'growing pains'. Now she felt as if she were being stretched to hold this one. This was not exactly a pain, though it hurt. It ached, but it was not like the ache she had had with dysentery, it was not sore, and it was not like toothache, that awful toothache she had when her tooth fell out. Analysing her pain, it began to go away, and she immediately forgot what it had been like.

Every family has its milestones; the first teeth come and the first teeth go; there is the first short hair-cut, the first braces, the first number one shoes, the first birthday in double figures. Events happen, too, which change families and family relations, and sometimes, often, one member is struck at more than another. Now, this feeling of pain, of hurt, had come to Harriet. This winter strange things seemed to be happening to her, eventful things. She felt herself growing and growing as she sat there in the gloom of the Secret Hole.

But soon she had regained her halcyon insouciance.

'Har-ee!'

'He-ah.'

'Get the scissors quick. Ram Prasad says the goldfish

should have a worm and here is a worm, Harry. Cut him into bits, quick.'

'Harriet,' said Bogey, as they fed the fish. 'What do you think, Harry? The cobra comes out into our side of the garden now.'

'*Bogey*!' said Harriet appalled. 'Have you seen it?'

Bogey nodded. His face was illumined.

'Wha – what is it like?'

'It is lovely. It slithers.'

'Ugh!' said Harriet, and she asked, 'How did you make it come?'

'I did what they did. I put down saucers of milk.'

'Ugh!' said Harriet. 'Oh Bogey!' and a quiver of sense, an antenna, lifted and pointed. 'Now I ought to tell Father. It is *in* the garden now.'

'But it is hardly ever in it,' said Bogey, earnestly. 'You can't say it is, Harriet. It lives the other side of the tree. That is where its hole is. It hardly ever comes out. Sometimes I watch for ages n'ages and it doesn't come.'

'Does Ram Prasad know?'

'No,' said Bogey absently. 'I don't *touch* it, Harry.' He added gently to himself so that even Harriet did not hear, his eyes bright and dreaming, 'I only poke it with a little bit of stick.'

Harriet was really too interested in herself to think about the cobra. She was hurt again. She was often hurt now. Things hurt her that would not have hurt her before, that she would have skimmed over without noticing. She was different. She was altogether puzzled, and on the afternoon of the second day she went to talk to Bea.

Bea was reading.

'Bea.'

Bea looked up. Her book was one of those books of Valerie's, *The Girls Own Annual* or *The Rose Book for Girls*, books that Harriet was not addicted to. Harriet liked *The Orange Fairy Book* and *Arabian Nights*. Or did she? Did she like anything? 'Bea,' she said, and Bea looked up but kept her finger on her place to let Harriet know that the interruption was to be only temporary, and Harriet, with Bea in that mood, could not talk about the nebulous things she had come to talk of. She had to think of something else, something important, if only to rivet Bea's attention.

She said, 'I have lumps.'

'Lumps?' asked Bea.

'Yes. On my chest. You know, my two chests, like swellings, and they hurt.'

'Those are your two little new breasts,' said Bea, and went on reading.

'Mine? But ... I am too young.' Harriet shrank back into her frock. 'I am far too young,' she said, shocked.

'You can't be or they wouldn't come,' said Bea reasonably. 'They don't come until you are ready.'

That was interesting. Harriet looked down, inside her frock, at her chest. Her frock was of blue cotton and the light on her skin was therefore blue as well; her chest no longer had a plain bow; its topography had altered to two soft warm swellings, and in between them the skin was wonderfully tender, fine and silken. 'It is pretty,' said Harriet, looking down inside her frock. 'And my veins *are* blue. It isn't only the light.' That skin, those veins were older than Harriet. They were the sign of a woman. She was visibly growing. Were these signs something only for girls? she wondered, and she tried to think of something male which was a counterpart, a visible growth, like this, and she could only think of stags, of the antlers of a stag. 'I hurt rather like a stag,' she said. 'Like a stag's new antlers hurt. Have you got them, Bea?'

'What? Antlers?'

'Breasts.'

'Yes,' said Bea shortly.

'I never noticed them.'

'You never notice anything that isn't yourself,' said Bea, which was largely true, though lately Harriet was noticing in this new acute way.

'Bea.'

'Do go away, Harry. I want to read.'

'But I want to talk ... about you, Bea.'

'I hate talking about me.'

How odd, thought Harriet, who loved above all things to talk about herself.

It was true. Bea had slipped off from Harriet and a space was widening between them. They were still officially 'the big ones', while Bogey and Victoria were 'the little ones', but like most labels, these were not true. Harriet, if she played at all, played with Bogey nowadays, and the truth was, that the completeness went out of their play if Bea played too. 'Not in the doing games,' said Harriet to herself. 'She can still play those: rounders, and flying kites and "animal-mineral-vegetable".' They played rounders on the lawn with the young men from the Red House after a Sunday tea that had plum cake and chocolate tarts; for Harriet it always meant running when she was too full to run, Bogey had a curious inability to grasp what he was doing, Victoria was allowed to play by courtesy, but Bea really played, gracefully and competently. She was good at the game of flying kites too; that was, flying paper kites off the roof with strings glassed with ground glass, when you challenged other unknown kites, crossed strings with them and tried to cut them adrift; your kite wore a bob on its tail for every kite it cut. 'Animal-mineral-vegetable' was agony to Harriet, because she inevitably forgot in the middle and let her mind go off cantering free in questions of its own: What-would-I-feel-like-if-I-were-vegetable-scarlet-flower-flesh-or-if-I-were-silver-or-tin-with-tin-fingers-and-tin-toes-and-little-tin-ears-and-tin-hair? She saw her hair flashing with curls of shining tinfoil and, of course, she lost her place and Father called her a dunce. Bea was never a dunce at this, but she could not play 'being' games any more; being Rowena or a Cavalier, or Arabs or high-waymen or pirates, or even Minnehaha. Bea was still not bad as Minnehaha, not bad, but not really Minnehaha; it seemed she could not be anything but Bea just at present; and now ... 'Am I going to be like this too?' asked Harriet.

As Bea grew into being only Bea, she grew mysteri-ously better-looking. She grew beautiful.

'What a beautiful child,' people said when they saw her.

Harriet and Bogey went behind a bush to discuss whether or not they would tell this to Bea.

'We don't want to make her conceited,' said Harriet and she did not know herself why she said that.

'Oh, tell her. Tell her. Tell her,' begged Bogey.

When they told Bea she did not become conceited. She seemed simply to take it as her due and to be unmoved by it, in a way that made Harriet feel breath-less.

Now, as Bea was reading, Harriet took a long firm view of her. Over the edge of the bright blue-bound book, Harriet was impressed again by the withdrawn look on Bea's face, by its shape, oval and clear, with the clear modellings of the cheekbones under their soft skin, her straight small nose, and the fine lines of her eyebrows; as she read, looking down, her lashes were spread, fine and curled, along her lids, and her dark hair fell on to her shoulders. Round her neck, on a black ribbon, she was wearing a carved ivory rose, tinted pink; her skin was tinted in exactly the same way, pink on ivory.

Harriet went away and looked at herself in the glass.

'What are you doing, Harriet?' said Mother.

'I am wondering if I am as beautiful as Bea,' said Harriet.

'You have a little face full of character,' said Mother kindly, 'and you have nice eyes and hair.'

That means I am not, thought Harriet. She could see for herself that her face looked pink and commonplace after Bea's; it was speckled with freckles, it had a large nose, green-brown speckly eyes under tawny eyebrows, and something tawny and rampant in her hair. It is more like Bogey's face, thought Harriet. But no, it is not even as nice as Bogey's. Bogey has such dear little bones. He is more like Bea, really. No, mine is nothing, nothing at all, like hers.

'Why do I want to be pretty suddenly?' asked Harriet, and she did not know. Certainly she had never bothered about it before, but then she had never bothered about anything very much. What is the matter with me? thought Harriet. Why do I keep on having these ... cracks? Why is everything suddenly so funny?

She was unhappy again in rifts, in, as she called them, cracks: for ten minutes, or for a minute only, or for a whole half hour. 'It isn't fair,' said Harriet in a temper, 'for a family not to be the same. To be half ugly and half pretty, to grow up at different times,' complained Harriet. With all she felt, and truly felt, another part of her was watching and found it interesting. She watched herself when she went to brood in the Secret Hole, when she went to sit on the jetty or under the cork tree. 'I give up,' said Harriet crossly, but the other part of her was far too interested to give up.

Meanwhile she was separating from Bea. Bea had passed into a kind of upper society with Valerie or Captain John. Harriet used to overhear them talking; she listened, not to Valerie of course, but to Captain John.

'What is the name of those flowers?' He was always asking Bea the names of flowers. He did not appear to be able to remember any for himself, or to know the commonest flower names. He went on asking them. I believe he likes doing it, thought Harriet, and she marvelled that Bea never lost patience or let him know she knew he was pretending.

'What is the name of those flowers?'

'Petunias,' said Bea.

He bent down to smell one. 'They remind me of you,' he said to Bea. 'No, you remind me of them, one of those purple ones,' he said, 'or a white one.'

Bea took it with the same calmness, almost with primness, but Harriet was dizzy. They are both behaving like grown-up people, she thought indignantly, or they are both behaving like children. Why? And then Captain John turned and said, 'Why don't you go away and play, Harriet. Don't tag on to me all the time.'

Harriet became scarlet to the tips of her ears. 'I don't ... tag,' she said in a muffled voice. 'I was only here, that is all,' and she rushed away, up the side stairs to the Secret Hole and cast herself down on the floor. 'I hate him. I hate him,' said Harriet, again, crying into the floor.

Her tears fell into the dust and it mingled with the tears on her face. When she came out Nan said she was not fit to be seen, and made her have her tea in the nursery.

'I warned you,' said Nan.

Harriet hunched her shoulders.

'If I were you,' said Nan, 'I should keep to playing with Bogey.'

'I am too big to play with Bogey,' said Harriet angrily.

'You are too small for Captain John,' said Nan.

More and more Harriet was thrust with Bogey, and this meant, usually, being alone. Whatever she started to do with Bogey, he eventually and cheerfully left her alone. After a few minutes, she would look up, and there would be no Bogey.

They were beginning to find that out in lessons. Bogey had just started lessons. 'He really must learn to read,' said Mother. 'It is disgraceful, at his age, not to be able to read.'

Why had no one taught him to read before? Because

he defied them completely. Yet he was not naughty. He was perfectly docile.

'M.A.T. Bogey?'

'Mat.'

'F.A.T. Bogey?'

'Fat.'

'C.A.T. Bogey?'

'Cat.'

'R.A.T. Bogey?'

'Sailor' and Bogey was entirely absent. Nor could they get him back.

'Why did the Ancient Britons find it so hard to make their boats, Bogey?'

'Because they had to make the inside bigger than the outside,' said Bogey gravely, his eyes on the sky.

He was not capable of being made to feel guilty, like Harriet, who knew she dreamed. He simply removed himself, and they were tired of the chase long before he was caught.

'One day you will have to learn to read,' said Harriet. 'Imagine a man who couldn't go to the office, nor sign letters, nor read newspapers.'

'I am not going to be any of those men,' said Bogey. 'I am not ready to learn to read.'

'You can't always do what you like, you know,' said Harriet, who was still feeling sore and angry.

'I can,' said Bogey. 'I always do.' That was true. He always did, and if he found trouble he kept it to himself. Once he fell down the back stairs and broke his front teeth. He never told anyone till Nan saw his swollen lips. Once he set his sock alight when he was cooking on a secret fire. He put out the sock and tied a rag on the burn. He never told. It was of no use. Bogey was no companion. Harriet still needed Bea. She could not, in any ultimate move, do without Bea. Bea still had to be her mentor, her help and her confidante, her guide and her public opinion. She tried to bid for her attention; or now, better than Bea, Captain John.

She painted a picture; it was of a lotus on blue water, and when it was done, looking at it critically, she could see that it was nothing like a lotus, it was more like a pig in bluish mud. She did not show that to Bea. 'I am not a painting person,' said Harriet. 'I am a writer,' and she tried for a little while to recapture the status of the poem she had written under the cork tree; she wrote a book, at least the beginnings of a book, and it kept her happy for some days. Then she showed it to Bea, who had not any great desire to look at it.

And they had four children, read the reluctant Bea, *called Olive, Bice, Emerald and Spinach, all green as grass and slimy.*

'Queer children!' commented Bea.

'This is a book about frogs,' said Harriet huffily.

'Well, you should say so.'

'You are supposed to understand that from reading the book.'

'Well, *I* didn't,' said Bea.

It was no good. This was a thoroughly tiresome time, and Harriet could not do anything with it.

It was nearly Christmas. 'It must be a quiet Christmas,' said Mother, as she had said about the winter. 'A quiet Christmas, and you must be content with little presents.'

The war again, thought Harriet angrily. She wanted Christmas to have its full panoply, she wanted the right to be happy and excited without this horrible onus of caring about other people, the hungry children, the wounded soldiers, the women left without husbands and fathers. 'And even if there isn't a war, it is just the same,' she said. 'There are always hurt people and starved people, and beaten people and misery.'

'And there are always the people who don't care,' said Bea.

'Well, I care really. I have to,' said Harriet.

'Of course you care,' said Captain John, and he smiled kindly at her. Now Harriet came to think of it, he did not often smile, and when he did … Why, he most often smiles at me, thought Harriet dazzled. Not at Bea, nor Victoria; at me, at something I say or do. It is as if he couldn't help smiling then. Yes, I am the one who makes him smile.

'Do you ever feel you want to fight again, Captain John?' asked Valerie.

'No,' said Captain John curtly.

'When I am grown up,' said Harriet, 'I am not going to fight in wars. I am going to fight the people who make wars.'

'Is that any better?' asked Bea. 'Everyone seems to be always fighting and fighting, and it doesn't do any good. If I were a man, I should be one of those people who say they won't fight.'

'I wonder if you would,' said Captain John.

'Why, didn't you?' asked Bea. It was seldom she asked a point-blank question, especially of Captain John, and he answered it with the seriousness it deserved.

'I wanted to ... but I couldn't trust myself.'

'How – not?' asked Harriet, puzzled, 'if you wanted to.'

'At the last pinch,' said Captain John, 'at the last pinch I think I should have been angry and fought to save myself – and it is no use unless you can go through that last pinch.'

They did not understand.

'But what good does it do?' asked Bea. 'Fighting?'

'Well, that is not the only point,' said Captain John slowly.

'Why not? What other point could there be?'

'It is something,' he said, 'to believe enough to die for that belief. Perhaps it is more than something, perhaps it is everything – to – aspire – to try.'

'Yes,' breathed Harriet. 'Like martyrs.'

'I think the martyrs were stupid,' said Bea. 'I think soldiers are too. Fighting is stupid.'

'Perhaps it is,' said Captain John. 'But perhaps that is neither here nor there. Perhaps the thing is, to believe.'

'And get killed for it?'

'If necessary.'

'I think so,' said Harriet. 'If I were brave enough ... only I wouldn't be,' she said. 'But I believe in things.'

'Oh you!' said Valerie. 'You will believe in anything.'

'That is better than believing in nothing,' said Captain John.

'Is it?' said Bea.

'Yes.'

'I don't think so,' said Bea.

'I do,' said Captain John.

Harriet stared at them. They were quarrelling.

They had been having tea in the garden, in fact Victoria, who ate inordinately, had still not finished and Nan was pouring out more milk for her. Harriet had left the table early and come to stand under the cork tree, listening to the woodpeckers, while she decided what she would do with the rest of the afternoon. Bea came after her, Captain John came after Bea and Valerie had brought a chair for Captain John. Valerie's fussing and homage annoyed him. It was true it took him ages to lower himself on to the grass, but it is better to let him take ages than to notice him, thought Harriet, and now, he held on to the chair and deliberately let himself down to sit with them on the grass.

Harriet began to build a fence of twigs. Somewhere, in the distance, she could hear Bogey hallooing. Bea sat with her legs curled under her, sitting sideways into her white skirts that were patterned with a pattern of old rose sten-cillings. Harriet's dress was the same, except that it was patterned with China blue; that difference changed its whole character, it looked merely crisp and fresh, while Bea's ... 'looks like ... poetry,' said Harriet. Why are some colours filled with poetry and others not? 'Why can't *I* choose my clothes?' she had said to Mother. 'Why can't I wear what I like?' 'Now Harriet,' began Mother, 'you are very nicely and suitably dressed ...' Harriet sighed.

The quarrel was continuing.

'Your ideas are so ... unsteady,' said Bea to Captain John. Once more they were like two children, or two grown-ups, and that isn't Bea's word, thought Harriet. She learnt that from Father. 'So ... unsteady,' said Bea.

'Are they?' said Captain John. 'Once they were burn-ingly steady.'

That silenced Bea and moved Harriet. She stopped her play with the twigs and put her hand on his knee. It was the knee of his artificial leg, but he seemed to feel it. 'Won't they ever be again?' asked Harriet.

'No. I don't think they will,' he said, looking down at her hand. It was a little dusty from the twigs, but he did not tell her to take it away.

'I think they will,' said Harriet.

'Valerie,' said Bea getting up, 'come and practise,' and she and Valerie walked away, arm-in-arm, linked together. Presently the not-quite-synchronized sounds of their new duet came down to the garden from upstairs. Harriet looked down at the grass because she knew that Captain John cared. The silence, broken only by the duet, grew too long.

'You shouldn't care,' said Harriet severely, speaking into the grass. 'You are a man and she is a little girl.'

'If I were ninety and she were nine, or the other way round, it would be all the same,' said Captain John. She could hear him breathing.

'Do you – love her?' asked Harriet, digging with her finger in the grass.

'Yes and no,' said Captain John. 'Never mind, Harriet,' and he added, 'There are some things you understand better than Bea,' and he said, speaking lightly, 'We can't change her.'

That was true. Bea would not change. Under her charm and softness she was adamant, and people never guessed how adamant she was because she was resilient. 'I expect you find Harriet the difficult one,' they said to Nan, and Nan shook her head and pursed her lips. With the deadly knowledge that old servants have, Nan could have told a thing or two of Bea, though she never did. 'Bea is by far, far, the most difficult,' was all that Nan would say.

'She knitted more Red Cross scarves than any of us,' said Harriet now, and then she added truthfully, 'But it was because she wanted to be the best at knitting,' but she did not say that aloud because after all Bea was as good a sister as could be expected.

She tilted her head and looked up through the branches of the cork tree to see the clouds moving and the house and tree tilting back against the clouds.

'Funny,' said Harriet to herself. 'The world goes on turning, and it has all these troubles in it.' She looked down the garden to the tea-table, where Victoria still sat. Horrible-wounds-and-milk-and-bread-and-butter-and-loving-and-quarrelling-and-wars. What was a quarrel but a little war? And there were wars all over the world. They have even come in here, thought Harriet, looking at the big stone house that was her home. But, thought Harriet, this *is* the world.

The sound of playing had stopped and there was no sign of Valerie and Bea. That probably meant they had gone up on the roof; the roof was a favourite place for walking or pacing; its flatness and its four parapets like walls were restful; there you could not see anything but the sky and the hawks circling and a few bright dots of paper kites. If you climbed up on the parapet, of course, you saw the whole wide vista of the land: town-river-boats-trees-works-Ram-Prasad's-little-house-by-the-gate-the-faraway-temple-another-temple-across-the-river, thought Harriet. Climbing up on the parapet was forbidden, but she and Bogey climbed.

Every family has something, when it has left home, that is for it a symbol of home, that, for it, for ever afterwards, brings home back. It may be a glimpse of the dappled flank of a rocking-horse, a certain pattern of curtain, of firelight shining on a brass fender, of light on the rim of a plate; it may be a saying, sweet or sharp, like: *'It will only end in tears.'* *'Do you think I am made of money?'* *'It is six of one and half a dozen of the other'*; it may be a song or a sound; the sound of a lawn-mower, or the swish of water, or of birds singing at dawn; it may be a custom (every family has different customs), or a taste: of a special pudding or burnt treacle tart or dripping toast; or it may be scent or a smell: of flowers, or furniture polish or cooking, toffee or sausages, or saffron bread or onions or boiling jam. These symbols are all that are left of that lost world in our new one. There was no knowing what would remain afterwards of hers for Harriet.

Being European in India, the flavour of Harriet's home was naturally different from most; it was not entirely European, it was not entirely Indian; it was a mixture of both. The house was a large oblong of grey stucco, flat-roofed, its parapet ornamented with those improbable daisies. The river ran past its garden and the tree rose high in front of its serpentine drive.

It was a double-floored house, with long verandahs. The rooms were all high, cavernous, stone-floored and whitewashed; shaded by the verandahs, they were always dim, though the end rooms had green-shuttered windows. For nine months of the year electric fans moved the upper air. They did not at first appear the kind of rooms that made a home, but Harriet's home was a peculiarly pleasant place.

On the ground floor was the dining-room, red-floored, pillared, with large pictures in large frames, reproductions of Gainsboroughs, Reynolds and Romneys. The dining-table was oval and capable of taking extra leaves; at night it had an embroidered cloth and pink-shaded candelabra above its bowl of roses or pink sandwich creeper; those candles always woke excitement in

Harriet. There was also a barrel, hooped with brass, that had once held salt meat on a sailing ship; now it was used for drinks and the children could just manage to raise the lid and all of them, often, had small secret swigs. There was the high chair that even Victoria had outgrown, and there were Father's silver cups, won by his charger Maxim when he was a younger man in the Bengal Volunteer Horse; there, too, were all the children's christening mugs.

On one side of the dining-room was Father's room; it had his desk, papers, cupboards, his two guns, the telephone and Sally's, his fox-terrier's, basket. At the other end of the house on the ground floor was the double nursery with its battered furniture, the children's own personal bookshelves and small wicker armchairs and the Millais pictures that had been in Mother's nursery. Nan's bed, Bogey's and Victoria's cot were at the back of the room in a row and there was an ironing-board where the iron seemed perpetually heated. Nan's red lamp burnt in front of the holy picture over her chest of drawers; she always kept a sprig of jasmine in her vase. The guinea-pigs' cage, the rocking-horse and the scooters that no one ever touched, were out on the verandah.

Upstairs was Mother's bedroom where she and Father slept and where anything private and serious in the family was discussed: 'talks', and what Mother called 'reasoning' and whippings; temperatures were taken there, the doctor examined throats and chests and ears and stomachs. Harriet, Bogey and Victoria had all been born in that bedroom.

Next door was Harriet's and Bea's room and their two white beds from which they talked at night; next door to that again was the drawing-room.

The drawing-room was always confused for Harriet; there were so many things in it, both objects and happenings, that she could never remember it exactly. It was a large room and one end of it was left almost bare, with its green floor holding only the piano and the music rack and a tiger skin with a snarling head on the wall. The other end of the drawing-room was furnished very thoroughly with chairs and couches, bookcases and a cabinet, a fireseat and, in the centre, a low brass tea-table on carved wooden legs. The tea caddy was tortoiseshell and very old; it stood on the mantelpiece with the Worcester cups and a tiny Dresden china cup that belonged to Bogey. Harriet never knew why it should belong to Bogey. Mother's writing-table held a pile of account books, and notes, and catalogues. There was a sweet-pea chintz on the chairs and real sweet peas in bowls, or else sweet sultans and gypsophila, or else, when it was getting hot, vases of tuberoses. There were small rubbed leather books that were sets of the classics, Scott and Thackeray and Dickens, and there was a scrapbook made for Harriet's grandmother when she was a child. The cabinet held a compendium of games.

The house had three staircases, a main one of dark wood, a side one painted white under which was the Secret Hole, and a back one for the servants which the children were not allowed to use, though Bogey and Harriet used it. Double flights of stone steps led from the downstairs verandah into the garden at the front of the house. The kitchen and the servants' quarters were outside, and there were stables, a washerman's yard, an electric-light-machine shed, a garage, and the porter's, Ram Prasad's, house beside the gate.

'It is more comfortable than anywhere on earth,' Harriet would have said of her home. It had fitted her like her own skin, but just lately she had come to see it more critically and more clearly. 'Is it that I am getting old?' wondered Harriet. 'I am getting old, look at my little breasts. Or is it Valerie and Captain John?' And she added honestly, 'It is something to do with knowing Valerie and Captain John.'

Certainly, since she had known them, everything in the house had been thrown into sharper focus, but then they, particularly Captain John, had coincided in a curious way with her growing up. Had she grown up because of them? She could not tell, but she knew now, for instance, that her parents had not as much money as Valerie's. Her eyes had been opened to contrasts: Valerie's clothes and their own home-made handed-down dresses; Nan and Valerie's travelling governess; Harriet's family had no car, they had only one child's pony. 'When the cradles fill,' said Harriet's father, 'the stables empty.' Of course we do have a lot of children, thought Harriet, but we have no Persian rugs, no wine at dinner, no ice cream, and when we go for picnics we don't have a basket with plates and cups and everything to match. 'Yes. I suppose we are poor,' said Harriet. 'Compared to Valerie ... we haven't been anywhere, and we don't know anything at all.'

She felt crushed. Captain John raised his head.

'What is the matter, Harry?'

'I was thinking – of us – our family.'

'And what did you think of it?'

'Not very much,' answered Harriet.

'Then I will tell you what I think,' he said. 'I think you are the very best family I have ever known.'

'D-do you?'

'Yes, I do. And don't you forget it,' said Captain John.

Something fell with a small soft plop on Harriet's head. It was a cork-tree flower just breaking into cream petals from its bud.

'Look,' cried Harriet in an excess of happiness. 'Look. That means that it is nearly Christmas. The tree is always in flower for Christmas.' Her face clouded. 'But it can't be as good a Christmas this year,' she said.

'It may be the best you have ever had,' said Captain John.

Of the families who keep Christmas, some keep it rather more, some rather less. Harriet's family kept it implicitly.

Besides the cork tree, the chrysanthemums were always out for Christmas; their scent was a part of it, like the smell of the withering fir tree and of hot candle wax and raisins and tangerines. Any of those scents, for ever afterwards, filled Harriet with the brand of quivering excitement she had known as a child at Christmas.

Their Bengali Christmas had its own brand too; it was

always perfect weather, the weather of a cool fresh summer day. The day began the night before, as Bogey said, with carols and hanging up stockings; that led to the opening of stockings the next morning and early church in the Masonic Lodge (the town had no church) where the gardeners gave each person, even children, a bunch of violets wired with ferns. Then the merchants and clerks of the works and the district came to call on Father with baskets of fruit and flowers and vegetables and nuts and whisky and Christmas cakes decorated with white icing, tinsel and pink-paper roses. The servants' children came to see the tree and be given crackers, oranges and four-anna pieces. The young men from the Red House came to lunch and in the evening there was a Christmas tree.

All this happened every year, but there was, besides this, a thread of holiness, a quiet and pomp that seemed to Harriet to have in it the significance of the Wise King's gold. It linked Christmas with something larger than itself, something as large as ...? Harriet thought it was a largeness that had something to do with the river, that began as a trickle and ended in the sea. Afterwards she wondered if this feeling in Christmas came from Nan. This year, as the time drew on and there was much less of everything, less buying and hiding and writing and planning, it was there again and it was more pronounced.

Bogey did not want anything for Christmas.

'But you must,' said Harriet. 'You must have something. Mother didn't mean you to have nothing.'

'But I want nothing,' said Bogey obstinately.

'You can't want nothing. You must want something.'

'But I don't. I have what I want.'

'You must want new things,' argued Harriet.

'I don't like new things. I like what I have.'

'What have you?' Bogey did not know. 'You haven't anything. You buried all your soldiers.'

'If I get any more I shall bury those,' said Bogey darkly.

'Pooh! You only like insects and horrid snakes.'

'Harry,' said Bogey, his face changing. 'I have been thinking. You know how the snake-charmers play on their pipe things? Well, I am going to play on my whistle. You know my whistle that Captain John gave me? I am going to play like a charmer on that. My snake might like it.'

This was the season for snake-charmers. This was the time they came walking through the East Bengal towns and villages, black-skinned men with beards, dressed in dark orange clothes. They carried a pole on their shoulders, and from each end of the pole hung down a loop of cloth in which were round shallow baskets that would just hold the coils of a snake. Baskets were piled on baskets, but many of the snakes were great worms, harmless and thick and stupid, not like a cobra with its strong strike and beauty and interesting wickedness. Very often the snake-man would have a mongoose, tied around the neck with a cord, its little red eyes gleaming. The mongoose would be put to stage a fight with a snake. I wish we had a mongoose here, thought Harriet, and he would kill that cobra. 'I don't think you ought to play with it, Bogey,' said Harriet aloud.

'It – doesn't come now. I think it has gone,' said Bogey quickly, but he lied.

The snake-man's pipe was a pipe on a gourd that made a sound like a bagpipe, sinuous and mournful. Bogey's whistle sounded merely hopeful after it.

'Why do you want to whistle if it has gone?' said Harriet sternly.

His eyes flickered. 'Oh ... just 'cos.'

'If a snake-charmer hears about your snake,' said Harriet, 'he will come and take it away. They are always looking for cobras. You had better take care.'

'I should like to be a snake-charmer,' said Bogey dreamily.

Harriet was tired and cross with her own preparations, which were always elaborate and always caused her family a good deal of tribulation before they were given.

'And what are *you* giving, Victoria?' she asked.

'I?' said Victoria, surprised. 'Nothing.'

'But *Victoria*, you must give people things.'

'Must I?'

'Yes. You can't take things and not give them.'

'But I like taking, not giving,' said Victoria contentedly.

Bea had made a handkerchief for Captain John and hemmed it with even small stitches and competently embroidered his initials in the corner. 'But – I haven't anything nice to give him,' wailed Harriet.

'Why should you give him anything?' said Mother calmly. 'He is more Bea's friend than yours.'

Harriet knew that, but for some reason, to hear Mother say it, filled her with a storm of torment and rage. 'I – I – hate Bea!' she cried, but fortunately Mother had gone out of earshot and Harriet was left to swallow it alone.

All her auguries were for a miserable Christmas, but still that holy quiet persisted, even in her, and beside she had a secret, a secret iron in the fire. She tried to be gloomy about that too, but she could not; the warmth of her secret persisted in the quiet.

Every year Nan made a crib with a set of old German figures of the Nativity. They were of painted wood, older than Nan knew. Harriet could never see them without a great fascination, and now, when they were brought out of their boxes, ten days before Christmas, to stand in their cave of moss and sawdust lit by candles, Harriet's imagination was touched again. In her restlessness and unhappiness they touched her so deeply that a familiar urge rose up in her. 'I am going to write about them,' said Harriet suddenly. What shall I write about them? A Carol? A hymn? An Opera, thought Harriet modestly. Or an 'Ode to the Three Wise Men'? But there were so many odes.

There was a blue angel kneeling with a lap full of roses. Her legs and her face were salmon pink, she had a gilt halo with blue in its diadem and she was always the one Harriet remembered best, for the expression of pain and smugness on her face. She looked as if she had a remarkable headache. What is the matter with her? thought Harriet now as she had thought every Christmas. Is she too good? she wondered. Why does she pull that face? And an idea came to her and filled her mind, so that she went straight away into the Secret Hole and wrote down her idea in her book. It took most of the day, but when it was finished and she read it over, she was not surprised as she had been when she read her poem; she was tickled and delighted, as she had thought she would be. 'Good,' said Harriet, biting her pencil. (She bit her pencils so badly that Nan said her inside must be like the floor of a carpenter's shop.) Now, as she remembered to take her pencil out of her mouth, a second idea, an idea of what to do with her idea, came to her, and this was of such dimensions that she was dazzled. 'But – could I?' asked Harriet. 'How could I?' and she looked doubtfully at the pencil-writing in her round handwriting in the book. 'Could I?' and then her face and her voice hardened. 'I could,' said Harriet. 'I shall.'

Captain John was staying with them for Christmas. She went to find Captain John.

'Come into Father's office,' said Harriet to him. 'I want to speak to you.'

He obligingly came, but like Bea, he kept his finger in his book. 'Put your book down,' said Harriet. 'I need you.'

'But—' he said. 'But—' he said again when she had explained.

'It is no use saying "but",' said Harriet firmly, and she began to uncover Father's typewriter that she was forbidden to touch. 'You can type,' she said. 'You said you could. This must catch tomorrow's steamer. And you must write a letter for me too.'

'But – the *Speaker* is a grown-ups' paper,' objected Captain John.

'This is a grown-ups' story,' said Harriet. 'And they do put things like this in at Christmas-time.'

'Yes. But ... you are far too late. They choose articles for their Christmas number weeks before.'

'They may have kept a little space,' argued Harriet. 'And mine may be so much better than the things they have, that they may put it in after all.'

'That isn't very likely,' said Captain John.

'No, but it is possible,' said Harriet.

He put out his hand for her story as he had for her poem once before. Harriet gave him the book and waited, quiveringly expectant.

'*The Halo that was too Tight*,' read Captain John. He glanced up at Harriet with a twinkle in his eyes and down again. '*An angel complained that her halo was too tight.*' He read on and his lips twitched, and once he laughed.

When he had finished it he did not say anything, except, 'Very well, I will type it for you,' but he gave her shoulder a small squeeze.

'I expect I am a nuisance,' said Harriet humbly.

'Yes. You are,' he said, sitting down to the typewriter.

'I expect you will have to alter the spelling a bit, if you don't mind,' said Harriet happily.

'I expect I will,' said Captain John.

On occasions, very occasionally, things happen as you feel they will, as you feel in your bones they will. Once or twice more in her life, Harriet was to know that calm certainty, that power of will, and have it answered. She was quite right to be certain. There was a surety of touch in that small story; it was small to change, to crystallize and confirm, as it did, Harriet's whole life, but she had known it could not go wrong, and on Christmas morning, when the mail bag was brought in to Father as they were having breakfast, he stopped as he looked over the letters and said, 'Why, Harriet. There is one for you.' Then he looked at it more closely. 'It can't be for her,' he said. 'It is from the *Speaker*. There must be a mistake,' and he was raising his knife to slit it open when Harriet called out in agony, 'But it is for me. Don't open it, Father. It is for me. I . . . I am expecting it.'

Everyone turned to look at her.

Father, still doubtful, handed it to her, and now she learned what facing an inquisition meant; no one spoke;

they waited for her to open it. The envelope was buff coloured, addressed in typescript; in its corner was printed, *Speaker Ltd.*, *Speaker House*, *Calcutta*. The blood began to drum oddly in Harriet's ears. I-expect-I-am-sure-it-is-only-to-say-it-is-no-good-to-send-it-back, she thought rapidly to herself. She wanted to hide the envelope quickly in her hand and rush away with it and open it by herself.

'Go on. Open it, Harriet,' said Father. 'We are dying of curiosity.'

Harriet gave one appealing glance at Mother and opened it. A typed letter and pink cheque form fluttered out.

'*Harriet!* What have you been up to,' said Mother sternly.

'I haven't been up to anything,' said Harriet. 'I – I don't understand what it says.' And she burst into tears.

It was quite true. Father read the letter aloud, and then Captain John came limping in with a paper in his hand. Harriet's story had been there all the time in the folded Christmas edition of the *Speaker* by Father's plate. 'Well. I am absolutely damned!' said Father.

The rest of the day passed in bliss. 'I never want it to end,' said Harriet, and when it had run its full gamut it stayed, still perfect, in her mind. 'It will stay with me for ever,' she said. 'It is my new beginning. Today I have been born again,' said Harriet, 'as Captain John said.'

Father had cut the story out and pasted it into his scrapbook. He showed Harriet what he had written. *Harriet's first published work*, and the date. 'First!' With the feeling of elation there came to Harriet a feeling of responsibility. She had avowed herself. She had signed herself away. It was public now. She was different. With all the glory, she wished she could have kept herself a secret.

That night she could not sleep. She was too excited to sleep. She lay listening to the pulse of the steam escape and to the river; she looked out through the doors, where Mother had left the curtains looped, where the light was clear moon blue. There must be a moon, thought Harriet. I can see branches, but I can't see the top of the tree. I wonder . . . What she wondered she did not say. From Bea's bed there came the sound of a sob. She listened. There came another.

'Bea!'

Instant silence.

'Bea. Are you crying?'

Silence.

'Bea. You are crying.'

No answer.

Harriet left her bed and went across in her nightgown to Bea's. It was cold and Bea made no move to let her in, but she remained sitting on the edge of Bea's bed. It was shaken slightly up and down every second. Bea was crying.

'Are you – feeling sick?'

No answer.

'Is it – because – is it anything to do with today?'

No answer.

'Did anyone get angry with you?'

Only a shake in the bed.

'Is it Valerie?' asked Harriet angrily.

'No.'

'Is it … Bea, is it because I wrote the story and you didn't?'

'Of *course* not!'

'Is it – is it anything to do with Captain John?' said Harriet delicately.

Silence and complete stillness.

'What is it about him, Bea?'

'It is – it is—'

'You made up your quarrel, didn't you?'

'It – wasn't a – real – quarrel.'

'Shall I call Mother?' asked Harriet out of her depth.

'N-no. W-we mustn't d-disturb her. You kn-know that.'

'But you can't go on crying,' said Harriet.

Bea made an effort to be quiet. She sat up, but the sobs began again.

'Tell, Bea.'

'He ... he is ... going away,' said Bea, in a rush, without any breath.

'Is he?' said Harriet stunned. 'Going away,' and she went on repeating 'Going away. Going away,' till the words felt like two hammers hitting a sore place. 'Ouch!' said Harriet, wincing.

'Yes. He is going away. We sh-shan't see him any more.'

'No,' agreed Harriet. 'Then we shan't.' She sat on the bed feeling more sore, more than ever cold and separated. 'But not yet, Bea,' she said, 'not yet. Not now.'

'No, not yet,' said Bea, but she cried as hard as ever.

'Bea, don't cry so hard. Don't, Bea. He isn't going yet.'

'I am not crying because he is going,' said Bea. 'I am crying because ...'

'Because?'

'Because *it* is going,' said Bea in another rush.

'It? What "it", Bea?'

'It is all going so quickly,' said Bea. 'Too quickly. It is going far too fast.'

'Mmm,' said Harriet, beginning to understand.

'Much too quickly and too fast,' cried Bea. 'It is all changing, and I don't w-want it to change.'

'But it hasn't changed,' said Harriet. As she said that she knew that it was false. How much had changed even since this morning? Everything had changed.

'I like it to stay as it is,' said Bea. 'I don't want this to end, ever. I want it to stay like this always, but it won't.'

'No, it won't.' Harriet had to agree again sadly. There was nothing else for her to do.

'We can't keep it, and today was so l-lovely – happy.' Bea's head went down in her pillow again. 'I want to be like this for ever and ever,' she cried.

So did Harriet. She sat hurt and cold and silent on Bea's bed until Bea put out a hand to her. 'Don't you stay, Harry,' she said. 'There isn't anything we can do, you're c-cold. Your hand feels like a frog.'

Harriet crept, cold and helpless, back to bed, but long after Bea was quiet, she lay awake. She thought Bea was awake too, and this was the first time they had ever lain awake without talking. The day was gone. However they might lie awake and cry or ache, they could not claim it back again. Who was it who had said you could not stop days or rivers? Harriet could hear the river running in the dark, that was not really dark but moonlight. She shivered. In six or seven weeks perhaps he will go away. She tried to make herself believe that, but it did not seem, nor feel, true. What will Bea feel then? wondered Harriet. Will she feel worse than I shall? In books people are happy for ever and for ever. But those books are nonsense. Nothing is for ever and for ever, thought Harriet. It all goes away. But does it? Again she was struck by a doubt. Does it all go, be lost and ended – or in some way do you have it still? Could that be true? 'Is everything a bit true?' she had said to Captain John. Then she lost that hope. No. It is gone, thought Harriet. I didn't notice it before, but now I see. I see it – horribly. Why didn't I see it before? Because I was little? And aloud she said, 'Bea. Are you asleep?'

'No,' said Bea.

'Bea, does it show you are getting old?'

'Does what? I do wish, Harry, you wouldn't think in between the things you say. As Valerie says, how do you expect us to understand?'

Bea was cross, but Harriet persisted.

'What are the signs of getting old – like us?' asked Harriet.

'Lots of things I expect,' answered Bea wearily. 'Do you want to know now?'

'Yes.'

'Growing up, of course—'

'Growing pains?' asked Harriet.

'I suppose so. Learning more. Being more with Mother and less with Nan; not liking playing so much, nor pretending; understanding things more and feeling them longer; wearing liberty bodices; and oh, yes,' said Bea, 'I remember when we came down from Darjeeling this year, finding everything had grown far more little than I expected. When I went away it all seemed so big. When I came back, it was little; and I suppose,' said Bea slowly, 'being friends with Captain John has made me old.'

I am not so far behind all that, thought Harriet to herself.

Soon after that conversation with Bea, that talking of growing, Mother sent for them.

'Harriet and Bea. Mother wants to speak to you – in her room.'

'What about?' said Bea instantly and suspicious.

'She didn't tell me,' said Nan smoothly.

'But Nan knows,' said Harriet to Bea. Bea shrugged her shoulders.

It was January. The Christmas holidays were over and life had entered on the second lap of the cold weather. Lessons had begun. The begonia venustra creeper in the garden and along the front of the house was out in orange-keyed flowers. The cork tree had its full spread of blossom. There was, all day long, a smell of honey in the garden and of honey in the fields where the mustard was in flower. It was still cool; there were still cold morning mists that blew over the garden at dawn and gathered on the river. The excitement was all over. Life had settled to its tenor. Harriet's story, with other happenings, had lost its point of interest and been fined down by the passing of the days until now the family took it for granted.

'I want to talk to you,' said Mother. 'I think you are old enough to have this talk with me.'

Harriet, as a matter of fact, was not at all old that morning. She looked down, as she sat, at her brown scratched knees with their sprinkling of golden hairs, and at the shortness of her green-and-white checked gingham dress. The dress bore all the stains and marks of that morning's experiences: papaya-juice-from-breakfast-

Prussian-blue-from-painting-the-Sea-of-Azov-a-little-torn-hole-from-climbing-trees-a-long-mark-from-falling-down-while-chasing-Bogey-on-the-dewy-lawn.

Mother was looking at the dress too. 'What have you been doing, Harriet?'

Harriet hung her head. 'Playing.'

'A big girl like you! Perhaps you had better not stay,' said Mother. 'Perhaps you are not old enough. I will talk to Bea.'

Bea sat with a stony face, her shoulders hunched. She said nothing.

'Oh, Mother, please let me stay. I am old enough, really I am. It is only sometimes, when I play with Bogey. Mother, let me stay.'

Mother looked at Bea and Bea looked resentfully at the floor. Mother sighed. 'Well,' she said with another glance at Bea, 'perhaps you had better stay.'

Then there was complete silence, with only the regular steam puff from the Works and the steady sound of the river.

'You are getting to be big girls now,' said Mother.

Another silence. Bea sat stiff, withdrawn as far as she could be. Harriet began to be agog.

'Every day you grow a little more,' said Mother.

'Willy-nilly,' said Harriet suddenly.

Bea shot an angry glance at her from under her eyebrows, but Mother smiled. 'Yes, exactly,' she said. 'Willy-nilly. Soon, sooner than we guess perhaps, you, will become women.'

'Yes, I suppose we will,' said Harriet.

'I don't know,' said Mother, 'I have never asked you how much you both know about – life.'

'Life?' asked Harriet puzzled.

'Babies being born,' said Bea shortly, breathing through her nose.

'Everything,' said Harriet with certainty.

'Not only babies,' said Mother, and waited. Then she asked, 'You, Bea?'

'A little,' said Bea reluctantly.

'Well—' said Mother. She sighed again. 'We had better begin from the beginning . . . You know it is the women who bear the babies, carry them in their bodies – as I am doing.'

'Yes, Mother,' said Harriet, and she and Bea both averted their eyes from Mother.

'We – women have to make our bodies fit for that,' said Mother. 'Like a temple.'

'A *temple*?' asked Harriet, surprised.

'Yes,' said Mother. But still it did not seem quite certain, the idea did not quite fit.

'Because you see, Harriet, the bearing of children, for the man you love, and who loves you, is very precious and sanctified work.'

'Do you love Father?' asked Harriet immediately.

'Yes,' said Mother, 'I am glad to say I do.'

At that small statement, typical of her mother, the conversation became suddenly and intimately true. Harriet felt a surge of love for her. She put her hand on Mother's knee and Mother pressed her hand, but Bea still sat aloof, still as if she were angry.

Harriet was unable to prevent herself from talking, from forcing this on.

'But – having babies, doesn't it hurt – horribly?'

'Yes, it does,' said Mother. 'But nowadays they have so much to help you that you hardly feel the pain, at least, not very much. You needn't be frightened. The doctors are clever.'

'But – suppose there isn't a doctor. Suppose you were caught out in – the jungle – or a desert – or there was a *flood*!' said Harriet.

'Oh *Har-ri-et*! *Do* let Mother go on,' said Bea.

'To get ready this temple ...' said Mother, and her

voice sounded uncertain again as if she again had been thinking over how to put what she had to say, and was not sure of the result.

'To make it ready, changes happen in your body, when you are beginning to be big girls.'

'I know,' said Harriet, nodding. 'They have happened to me.'

Mother looked surprised and Bea impatient.

'You needn't snort at me. They have,' said Harriet.

'Yes, I expect they have. You are growing, but wait, Harriet,' said Mother. 'Listen.'

'Mother,' broke in Bea, '*must* we talk about this now? Can't we wait till this does happen? And *must* we have Harriet here?' She glared at Harriet as if she hated her.

And Harriet herself suddenly felt that she would prefer to postpone it, though she did not know why.

A sound came from the river, an approaching churning with a regular pulsing of engines. It was the twelve o'clock mail steamer. The noise grew louder as it passed the house, upstream, and then grew fainter; presently there came the sound of waves, its wash slapping against the garden bank. Mother, who had seemed to waver, gathered herself again.

'You can be patient for a few minutes longer,' said Mother. 'I shan't keep you long. It is always better for things to be talked of plainly.'

Bea looked as though she did not agree. 'And,' added Mother dryly as she watched Bea's face, 'it won't do you any harm to hear this from your mother, even if you have been told it by someone else already.'

She means Valerie, thought Harriet. Valerie has told her. Good for you, Mother, thought Harriet, refreshed to find how little of a fool her mother was.

Mother's eyes were resting on Bea's head as she began to talk again. Bea bent her head so that neither of them could see her face and her fingers picked, picked at the wicker stool she sat on. Why was Bea so funny, so resentful? And now Harriet found herself wishing that Mother would not keep them there, keep Bea, at any rate, there, to be talked at against her will.

But Mother talked on calmly and firmly, and soon Harriet forgot to look at Bea. She was listening with all her ears.

Mother's voice went steadily on. Then there was a third silence.

'Well!' said Harriet. 'Well!'

She looked down at herself, and it was true that she

was exactly as before, the same knees, the same hairiness, the dress with the same stains and marks. 'But – I didn't know what I was, what I am, what I am going to be,' said Harriet. For all she knew, had known up to now, she might have been the same as Bogey. Gone, and she thought regretfully of them for a moment, gone were some pleasing vistas she had seen for herself and Bogey; running away to sea and becoming cabin boys; turning into Red Indians, I should have to be a squaw, and I don't like squaws, thought Harriet; being an explorer, No, I suppose women are not really suitable for explorers, thought Harriet, they would be too inconvenient. And every month ... like the moon and the tides ... the moon brings tides to the world and the world has to have them ... it can't help its tides, and no more can I. All at once it seemed exceedingly merciless to the small Harriet, sitting on just such another wicker stool as Bea's in Mother's room.

'I wish I were Bogey,' said Harriet.

'I know,' said Mother. 'I often wanted to be a boy.'

'You?' asked Harriet in surprise. 'You did?'

'Yes I,' said Mother, 'but it is no good, Harry. You are a girl.'

But ... I don't think it *can* happen to me, thought

Harriet, and aloud she said, 'Mother, I don't think it will ...'

'Will what, Harriet?'

Bea made an impatient movement. 'That is what she always does, thinks, and then expects you to know what she is thinking.' It seemed to help Bea if she attacked Harriet. 'She is a perfect little silly. Can I go, Mother?'

'Bea ...' Mother began, but Harriet had to interrupt.

'To me? In *my* body? Are you sure, Mother?'

'I hate bodies,' burst out Bea, 'I want to go.'

'Very well then, go, Bea,' said Mother.

After Bea had gone, Mother sat still, and once again Harriet heard her sigh, but she herself was too engrossed with herself, with being Harriet, to feel this. 'I don't think,' she said, 'that I can be – quite an ordinary woman, Mother.'

'You will be the same as every woman when your turn comes,' said Mother, 'and so will Bea ... just as you said, willy-nilly. And now,' she said, 'perhaps you had better go back to your playing.'

'Play!' said Harriet. 'Play! I shall never play again.' But she did. The same day she was chasing Bogey on the lawn again.

*

In, the early afternoon, everyone rested. Father snatched an hour before he went back to the office, Mother rested monumental on her bed from two till four; Harriet and Bea read, Bogey was banished to a camp cot in Father's room, while Victoria slept and Nan sat in her chair in the darkened nursery and sewed under the window and sometimes dozed off. It was the servants' siesta time; even the birds were silent; even the lizards lay asleep in the sun.

If, however, Harriet had any pressing business she did not postpone it; she left her book and slipped off her bed and no one was any the wiser. 'I am going to rest in the Secret Hole,' she said to Bea. She was not, but Bea nodded quietly. Then Harriet went downstairs and almost always, as she passed Father's room, Bogey's camp cot was likewise empty.

This was Bogey's supreme time for his adventures, when there was no one to see him or hinder him or even be aware of him. It was the time, too, when the garden was least disturbed, when his insects and his reptile friends were most accessible. Harriet never remembered yet getting up and finding him in bed.

One afternoon, in late February, Harriet needed Bogey. She went downstairs to find him, but of course he was not there. She could not see him in the garden either as she stood on the verandah.

'Bother,' said Harriet, 'I shall have to go out,' and she went on tiptoe to the nursery to fetch her hat.

Nan was asleep. On her lap lay a pair of Victoria's knickers into which she was putting new buttonholes as Victoria grew too fat for the old; she still held her needle and her lips, as she slept, blew gently in and out. Harriet fetched her hat and went out.

She could not see Bogey anywhere. 'He is playing Going-round-the-garden-without-being-seen,' said Harriet, annoyed, and she began to follow him over the customary tracks that only she and Bogey knew. The garden was empty, brilliant with sun. Its colour blazed at Harriet. Here, as she went between the plinth of the house and the poinsettias, their flowers, as big as plates, long-fingered, scarlet, looked into her face as she passed; she half expected to see Bogey's face amongst them, Bogey's face screwed up in the sun, under his shock of hair. She crept between the poinsettias and the house just as he crept, but there was no Bogey there. He was not by the morning glory screen trumpeting its blue and purple flowers in the sun, nor under the swinging orange creeper at the house corner. He was not in the

bougainvillaea clumps nor anywhere near the rose turrets, nor under the jacaranda trees, nor by the tank.
Harriet went into the vegetable garden between the
rows of peas and white-flowering beans, and pushed
through the tomato bed, malodorous with its yellow
flowers, but he was not there. He was not in the stable
where Pearl stood looking stupidly out of her stall, half
asleep herself. Harriet stopped to pat her, to smell her
warmth, but Pearl did not alter her expression at all.
She only twitched her ear at a fly.

Bogey was not behind the little midden of manure, nor
in the servants' quarters where Harriet could see forms,
stretched out asleep on the string beds, under the trees
and the eaves of each hut.

She went behind the hibiscus standards, their flowers
hanging pink and scarlet and yellow and cream in lantern
shapes with tasselled stamens; she swung them as she
passed, but nothing else stirred or shook them. She went
where Bogey went, along the drain by the wall behind
the bamboos whose pipe stems stood, green and bronze
and canary yellow with only the sunlight filtering
between them. She went stealthily along expecting
Bogey to spring out on her with a cat-call any moment,
but the garden was as still and blank as ever. She went

into the fern-house and round the goldfish pond. Bogey was not there either.

Out on the open lawn, the sun beat down on the grass that had a haze of its own heat, and sent off a warm dry smell. All the scents of garden mixed with it, but still the scent of the yellow Marechal-Neil roses and of the petunias and of the cork-tree flowers was distinguishable. The lawn, too, was quite empty. The whole garden was empty, and Harriet flung herself down on the grass and looked back up at the house and the tree still making their journey against the sky. Far up the hawks still went round and round in their rings. They made her dizzy. 'I rather wish I had stayed in and had my rest,' said Harriet, yawning. 'I don't know where Bogey is. He plays "Going-round-the-garden" far too well. Probably he is here, quite close to me and laughing,' said Harriet crossly; but no, she had no feeling of Bogey being near and laughing. She had only a feeling of blankness, a complete blank. Blank, thought Harriet aridly, and yawned again. Blank.

All at once she sat up. I believe, she thought. I believe he is waiting for that snake. I believe he is by the peepul tree.

She did not want to go near the peepul tree; even the thought of the cobra made her spine go cold. 'Ugh!' said

Harriet. 'Ugh! I wish he wouldn't. I don't know how he can. I must tell Father. I am going to tell Father,' said Harriet, and she jumped up and dusted the dust of the grass off her hands and knees and elbows.

She went to the gate where the bridal creeper, over now, hung in a tangle of dried green. The gate was open a crack. That meant Ram Prasad was out. His house was empty. Harriet looked in as she passed, and saw his 'lota', his washing-pot, and his lantern and his green tin trunk painted with roses standing neatly under his bed; his coat hung from a peg, his cut-out pictures were pasted on the wall and in the corner, near his earth cooking-oven, were his brass platters, his spoon and his brass drinking cup and his hookah. They were all utterly familiar to Harriet; she had seen them all hundreds of times.

Now she had come to the space round the peepul tree. Here, where the earth was bare because of the peepul roots, there was an empty space like a courtyard edged and screened with bamboos. There was nobody there, not even the cobra; her eyes had looked at once quickly among the roots, under the bamboos, to see a dark heap, a sliding coil. There was nobody, nothing, and then the blankness ran up into the sky, her feet were clamped to the earth; she had seen something else. It was not Bogey;

not the snake, but an earthenware saucer of milk lying upset and broken on the ground near a small bamboo stick and, further off, towards the bamboos, on the ground too, Bogey's sun hat was lying by itself. 'He has been bitten,' said Harriet's mind distinctly as she stood there.

It – it came out for the milk and he touched it with a stick and it struck. It struck, and again the blankness ran into the sky into a long pause. Then close to her feet, lying on the ground, she saw Bogey's whistle.

With trembling legs she bent to pick it up, and as she bent, she saw him.

He was lying in the bamboos, only a few yards away, spread starfishwise as if he had flung, or tried to fling, his arms and legs away from him; he was lying on his face, his body drawn up from his arms and legs in a small heap. 'I see,' said that dreadful clearness in Harriet's mind, 'he would do that. Try and hide in the bamboos. He would go off to hide it, not tell – and then when it hurt,' and she knew snake bite was a terrible pain, 'why then, I suppose he couldn't tell. No one would hear him. There was no one near enough to hear.'

She went towards him on shaking legs. 'Bogey,' she said in a voice that was a croak, 'Bogey. Bogey.'

She went nearer, her eyes looking in and out of the bamboos, on the ground, near him, away from him. There was nothing there. Only Bogey on his face.

She looked down on him, at the seat of his shorts, old grey-blue linen, and at his rucked-up shirt that showed his naked back and his spine. His hands were clutched and filled with earth and bamboo bits, and his hair was dirty with them too. He must have rolled about in them, thought Harriet. Her throat grew dryer, her breath hurt, her neck was cold. 'Bogey,' she croaked. 'Bogey—'

There was a rustle in the bamboos behind her, and she jumped so that her skin tingled. It was a bird, a jay. It made a harsh whirring and clapped its wings and flew. Don't they do that when a snake is near, thought Harriet, and now, where she had been cold, she was wet. She bent and took hold of Bogey's foot in its sock and brown shoe and gave it a little pull. 'Bogey,' she tried to say. 'Boge. Bogey. Boge.'

She had not expected Bogey to answer, and he did not answer. He did not move, and she had not expected him to move. The – the warm is gone, thought Harriet. The side of his face she could see was scratched and the skin was blue.

'Blue?' asked Harriet numbly, staring down at him.

'Blue? Why should he be blue?' She went on saying that as she looked and looked and looked. She said it until she heard the gate creak on its hinge. Ram Prasad had come back.

Then she broke the quiet. She screamed louder than the jay. 'Look. Look. Look,' she screamed. 'Ram Prasad! Ram Prasad! *Sarpe. Sarpe.* Snake. Snake. Snake.'

In India, when anyone dies, it is necessary that they are buried at once, and by sunset of that same day Bogey was lying in the small cemetery where the trees that had honey-balls like mimosa dropped their pollen on the old graves and the new graves, on the short earth mound that was Bogey's, on the stone of the other boy, John Fox, piper, who was fourteen when he died, two hundred years ago.

With the resource that a small far-away town often shows, a coffin was found and made to fit Bogey by the carpenters in the Works. The Works were stopped; the coolies went home, but the clerks gathered in a silent and respectful throng just inside the gate. The firm's small launch, the 'Cormorant', left her moorings and came up to the jetty; from other jetties, up and down the river, other launches put out, and on them were people from the other Works, and flowers from the other gardens. The gardeners knew what ought to be done; without being told they cut all the white flowers, white petunias and roses and candytuft and dianthus and gypsophila. In Harriet's garden they sat in the shade making wreaths though no one told them, and they made a cross, too, of yellow roses.

'Why can't I go out? Why can't I go *out?* whined Victoria.

'Be quiet,' said Harriet.

'Hush,' said Bea.

People, ladies and gentlemen, gathered under the cork tree. Abdullah and Goffura, who also knew what should be done, carried out chairs and trays of tea, but no one of the family came down to speak to anyone; everyone sat or stood talking in low voices while the cork blossom, that was falling, dropped on their heads or into their cups of tea.

'We haven't had any tea,' said Victoria. 'I want some tea.'

'Hush,' said Harriet.

'Be quiet,' said Bea.

Why did all the people come? wondered Harriet. They came as if they had a right to come, as if it were their duty. Now Mr Marshall, who was wearing a grey suit, not whites as he usually did, came and stood talking with a set grave face. They had come for Bogey? Why? 'Why do – they – all come?' Harriet asked Bea.

'It is the custom,' said Bea. 'Bogey has to be buried.'

'Buried?' said Harriet startled.

'Yes. You know that,' said Bea.

Harriet knew. She had always known, but it had not come to her before. When you died, you did not belong to yourself, nor to your family; you belonged to custom, and places and countries and religions; even a small boy like Bogey. Harriet remembered Father telling her about the Registration of Births and Deaths, the birth and death of a citizen. 'Then Bogey was a citizen,' she said aloud.

They huddled under Bea's bookshelf, straining to listen, trying to see and not see.

'I want to go out,' said Victoria. 'Why *can't I go out?*'

Then Nan came in.

'Why are you not dressed?' said Nan.

'Dressed?' They stared.

'Yes. You always get dressed for the afternoon?'

'Yes – but – but—'

'You would think no one had ever taught you how to behave,' said Nan. 'Take off that dirty frock, Harriet, and go and wash your face. You too, Bea. Victoria, come here and let me unbutton you.'

'But are we – is – Bogey—'

'Bogey is dressed,' said Nan with dignity. 'The house is full of ladies and gentlemen. We must show them that we – we care for him. You will get dressed and then come with me.'

'Shall we – see him?'

'I don't want to see him,' said Victoria. 'Ayah says he is all black.'

Nan's face folded in on itself suddenly, the lines by her mouth and her eyes folded in, and she shut her lids. Then she picked up the brush and without answering began to brush Victoria's hair. When they were dressed she walked them out on the verandah, between more people who parted and made way for them, and into Father's room. It was very dim, but Nan had lit two candles on the writing-table. There was only Bogey's coffin there heaped up with flowers.

'I don't know what Mother would wish,' said Nan, 'and I cannot ask her, but I think you should *not* see Bogey. You must say goodbye to him here.'

They stood close in the candlelight, in the smell of flowers where again the roses were the strongest. Why again, wondered Harriet. When – in what age had she thought that before? Then Nan took them out into the garden, away from the people, by the river.

The river ran with no noise of steam from the Works. It sounded queer.

Father and Mr Marshall came from the house carrying Bogey in his coffin. They carried him down to the jetty and put him on the deck of the 'Cormorant' and the people followed with flowers, till there was a hill of flowers on the deck. Some of the flowerheads fell off into the river, and were floated down and away. Then the 'Cormorant' cast off from the jetty and backed and turned in a half circle to go upstream, and the other launches, with their people, cast off too, and followed behind. Each launch left a pointed wake in the water.

The river can't close over this, thought Harriet; then she seemed to see again in the water the handful of ashes that had been Ram Prasad's wife, and she remembered how they had been washed, round and round, gently, on the water, before the current took them away.

Now the launches had passed out of sight. The colours in the garden were deepening in late afternoon sunlight; it was nearly evening.

*

Pieces of the next two days broke through to Harriet.

They found and killed the snake, not one but two, two cobras. Harriet saw Ram Prasad stretch them out on the ground when they were dead, one five feet, the other more than four. Bogey had been bitten in the neck, the right side below his cheek, Nan said. 'He was quickly dead,' said Nan.

After the cobras were killed, Harriet began to be sick. She was sick on and off, all those two days. In spite of that there was no respite. There were still things to do. Nan told her to go and find all Bogey's toys. She was packing his things away, out of Mother's sight.

Harriet could not find any toys except an old arrow, thrown down and rusty; she knew where Bogey had buried his soldiers, but she let them stay buried; she found a mud garden under a tree, but you could not pack a mud garden. She wandered round the garden that was the same garden, not changed, not different, but she walked in it not thinking, not touching, merely walking.

There was no clergyman in the town. Mr Marshall had read the service for Bogey. In the evenings, Mr Marshall and Dr Paget came to be with Mother and Father. One evening Mr Marshall stopped to speak to Harriet who sat on the steps looking at the darkness, not thinking, only looking.

'I expect you miss your brother,' said Mr Marshall kindly.

The jackals howled far out on the lawn.

'Well, it is a good thing it wasn't Victoria,' said Harriet.

Mr Marshall seemed slightly taken aback. 'Why?' he asked.

'Victoria is afraid of jackals,' Harriet explained. 'Bogey isn't.'

Nan forgot to pack Bogey's toothbrush. When Harriet was having her bath she saw it still there: Bea, pink; Harriet, green; Bogey, red; Victoria, blue. Harriet stood up in the hot water and took Bogey's down.

'What are you hiding in your hand, Harriet?'

When Harriet showed, Nan turned her back and tidied the towels on the rack.

'You can't keep that, Harriet,' she said.

'No,' Harriet agreed forlornly.

She put her head down on the zinc edge of the bath. Nan stayed by the towels, smoothing them down.

'We don't need to keep things, Harriet.'

'No,' said Harriet, not agreeing; then, as she relinquished the toothbrush, it was true. The less she had of Bogey, the more clearly she saw him.

There began to be shoots of life. Whether they were wanted or not, there were shoots of life.

Father went back to the Works. Mother came downstairs. Harriet heard her ordering the meals again. 'Soup. Celery soup with cream,' said Mother, 'mutton, mint sauce, peas, the garden peas.'

'Roast potatoes,' said the cook, entering it in Hindi in his notebook. He was an educated cook.

'Then orange baskets,' said Mother, and Harriet found herself chiming in, 'Yes. Can't we have orange baskets too, Mother? For our supper?'

Victoria made herself a new kind of house on the verandah table. She said it was a 'think house'. It was nothing but Victoria herself sitting on the table. 'Where are the walls? The roof? The front door?' demanded Harriet.

'It is a think house,' said Victoria.

'You mean you think it is a house, and it is?'

Victoria nodded.

'But what can you *do* with it?' asked Harriet.

'You can think in it,' said Victoria, with dignity.

Lessons began again. Lessons with Mother, with Father. Eating-sleeping-getting-up-going-to-bed-resting-washing-brushing-and-combing-and-doing-your-teeth-reading-swinging-riding-Pearl-knitting. All the outward things went on. Surprisingly, the inward things began to go on too. Nothing had changed. But everything, Harriet thought, has shrunk. Everyone has shrunk somewhere inside themselves, as if they are hiding and you are afraid to find them because you are afraid of what you may find. Occasionally, you would discover Mother cutting roses, stooped and picked up a lead Highlander off the path. It was one of Bogey's soldiers that Sally had dug up. Mother went indoors, dropping her scissors and the roses she had picked on the verandah table.

Harriet came into the nursery and there was Nan just as before, making buttonholes for Victoria. Harriet stopped, and her sickness came back again.

'What is it, Harriet?'

'Is is so – horrid – so cruel,' Harriet burst out.

Nan went on with her sewing.

'Going on and on. We go on as if nothing had happened,' wept Harriet.

'No, we don't,' said Nan. 'All we do is to go on. What else are we to do, Harriet?'

'It is as if we had wiped Bogey away. Look at you, making *button*-holes!' wept Harriet.

'What do you think I should do?' asked Nan quietly.

'That is just it,' Harriet could not hold her tears. 'It

happens, and then things come round again, begin again, and you can't stop them. They go on happening, whatever happens.'

'Yes, they go on happening,' said Nan, 'over and over again, for everyone, sometime, Harriet.'

Harriet sat down on the floor, and wiped her eyes on the back of her hand. She felt hollowed with her unhappiness, and then, as she sat there, leaning against Nan's chair, another astonishing shoot came up in her mind. 'No,' said Harriet, horrified at herself. 'No. No, I can't. I mustn't. *Write* about this? No. No. I can't,' but it was already forming inside her head, as Nan stitched buttonholes again, and again she heard the sound of her life, the steam puff-wait-puff and the river. It was true; on the surface, even deeper, it was all exactly and evenly the same.

The world goes round.

No, thought Harriet, trying not to listen to herself; it carried her on.

The river runs, the round world spins.

Dawn and lamplight, thought Harriet. *Midnight. Noon.* She shut her eyes and said it over to hear, in the old familiar way, if the words ran. It seemed to her that they ran properly and she went on:

> *The river runs, the round world spins.*
> *Dawn and lamplight. Midnight. Noon.*
> *Sun follows day. Night, stars and moon.*

The customary happiness and suspense and power filled her. She felt lifted again, as if she were rising up. She was ashamed, she tried to crush the words down, but they could not keep down. They insisted on rising.

> *Sun follows day. Night, stars and moon*
> *. . . the end begins.*

'Nan,' said Harriet, shocked.

'Yes, dear?'

'Nan, how can I be happy? How *can* I.'

If surprising things came out of Harriet, no surprises ever came out of Nan.

'It isn't for us to dictate, Harriet.'

'Oh Nan!'

'That is so,' said Nan, snipping her thread. 'If you are happy, you are. You can't make yourself unhappy. We are something, part of something, larger than ourselves, Harriet.'

Harriet was silent, remembering Christmas, and how

little she had felt below the stars, remembering Bea and what Bea had said about growing smaller as you grew older, only perhaps Bea meant that this otherness grew larger; she thought suddenly of the fish that the kingfisher had taken out of the river and of the splash it had made and of how the splash had gone and the river, with its other fish, its porpoises, its ships, had gone on running on.

Then what is the good of my writing my poem, thought Harriet, if it is all so big and I am so small? It wouldn't make a mark as big as a – a fly's leg against the whole world. I shan't write anything.

The river runs – it immediately began again.

'I have to go to the Secret Hole, Nan,' said Harriet, jumping up from the floor. 'I have a poem that I have to write down.'

But when she reached the Secret Hole, her box was empty. Her book was not there.

She came downstairs, hurtling down, and there was Valerie reading her book on the lawn.

'What are you doing with my book?' Harriet was scarlet.

'Reading it,' said Valerie, absolutely cool. Bea was standing by as if she did not quite know what Valerie was doing; she made no attempt to stop her reading Harriet's book, and worst of all, Captain John was reading his own book near lying on the grass.

'Give it to me.'

'No, I shan't,' said Valerie, turning over a page. 'I think it is very funny. Listen, Bea: *When I have thoughts they hum. I might have I think a little top in the top of my head—*'

'Bea. Make her give it to me.'

'Valerie. It is Harriet's private book.'

'Yes. I should think so,' said Valerie giggling. 'How could you, Harriet? There are all kinds of things in it. Captain John, here's one about you. There are a great many about you,' and she read out, *'I think that Captain John's face is like one of those plants that you touch . . .'*

'You are not to read it. You are not to,' screamed Harriet, flying at Valerie, but Valerie dodged away, nearer to Captain John, who had lifted his head to listen and look at them.

'Captain John's face is like one of those plants that if you touch roughly they shrink and close up. I think it is true. Father calls him a "sensitive plant". Oh, Captain John!' laughed Valerie, and Bea had to laugh too.

'You beast!' screamed Harriet. 'You beastly girl.'

'I think he is like Antinous whose face you never do forget,' read Valerie, dodging Harriet. *'Today I am so alive I am*

glad I am me and am born—' Valerie ended in a shriek as Harriet tore the book away and pulled her hair.

'Harriet. You mustn't hurt her.'

'She has hurt me,' shouted Harriet, 'the mean sneaking hateful beastly pig. How dare she.'

'I don't want to read your silly diary,' said Valerie, rubbing her shoulder where Harriet had wrenched her. She put back her hair and fastened her tortoiseshell slide that had come undone. Harriet hated her fuzzy brown hair and she hated her face, which looked considerably heated and a little uncomfortable. 'Why be so angry?' said Valerie lightly.

'It was her private book,' said Bea.

'She is quite right to be angry,' said Captain John, who with difficulty had risen from the grass and come to them. 'You had no right to take it, Valerie.' He looked almost as angry as Harriet, and Valerie saw that everyone was against her. She looked hotter than ever and her eyes grew bright with spite.

'I don't see why *Harriet* should be so haughty,' said Valerie, 'when everyone knows it was her fault Bogey died.'

It was said.

There was complete silence in front of the steps,

except again, in this pause, the steam puff and the river. Then Harriet turned and ran upstairs.

No one had spoken very much to Harriet about the cobra. She knew and they knew, and they knew that she knew. Father had questioned her. Her face and her voice had shown him how guilty and wretched she was, and he did not punish her. 'What,' said his whole attitude as he turned away, 'is the use of punishing now?' and that had twisted Harriet's heart more than any words.

Mother had said nothing either till Harriet had come and stood in front of her. 'Mother – I – I knew about – the – the – cobra – Mother.'

'Yes, Harriet. 'I know you did,' said Mother.

'Mother – I—'

'It is no use talking about it now,' said Mother.

There had been shocks. Ram Prasad was sent away. 'But why?' demanded Harriet. 'Why? He only knew it was there. *He* didn't know that Bogey—'

'There is no excuse for Ram Prasad. No excuse at all,' said Nan hardly.

Ram Prasad was, later, forgiven and reinstated, but that had given Harriet a glimpse of how people felt. Did they, then, think as hardly of her? She had only, so far, thought hardly of herself. Now Valerie's words burnt into her. *Everyone knows. Everyone knows.*

Harriet lay on her bed, her face turned to the wall.

Nan came in.

'Harriet,' said Nan.

'Please go away.'

'Harriet,' said Nan, 'I think you should get up.'

'I – can't.' Harriet's voice was muffled.

'You will have to get up some time,' said Nan reasonably, 'so I should get up now.'

'I can't, Nan. How can I?'

'With a girl like Valerie,' said Nan, 'a spiteful girl, you have to be very proud. You should not let her see she can hurt you.'

'It isn't only Valerie,' cried Harriet in despair. 'You didn't hear what she said. Oh, Nan, does everyone know? Does everyone say – *that?*'

'I expect they do,' said Nan calmly. 'You have to expect that because it is partly true, Harriet.'

'Yes, but – *who* could have thought—'

'You could have thought,' said Nan. 'You didn't use your sense. You know you didn't, and for that a cruel lesson has been given.' Her voice trembled and she looked with indescribable pity at Harriet, but she went on. 'Very cruel, but perfectly just,' said Nan. 'You can't complain about it. You must not.'

'What am I to do? What can I do?' cried Harriet.

'It is a thing that will have to pass away from you, Harriet.'

'It never will, Nan. Never! Never!'

'Yes, Harriet, it will,' said Nan. 'You have plenty of courage and you are strong. I have faith that it will,' and she pressed Harriet gently on the thigh and said, 'Get up now and face that Valerie.'

She rustled gently out, but Harriet did not get up. She lay on her bed engulfed with misery. All the sounds of the late afternoon came up to her and she could identify each one, but she lay cut off from them all. 'I feel as if I had thorns in my heart,' said Harriet. 'How hard Nan is. How hard,' she said. Now she could not be unhappy for Bogey by himself any more. Mixed with him, irretrievably, was the guilt and indictment, public not private, so that they were not by themselves any more. 'I wish I had died with Bogey,' whispered Harriet.

There was a knock on the shutters behind the curtain.

'Harriet, can I come in?'

'Captain John!' cried Harriet, shrinking in her bed.

'Yes. Can I come in?'

'No. Please no.'

'I am coming in,' said Captain John.

He came in. Made dim by the shadow of the room, he looked large, his movements very jerky. Harriet could not see his face.

'I have brought your book,' he said, and laid it at the foot of her bed.

'Thank you.'

She did not move. She did not want him to see her face.

'Don't you want it?'

Harriet shook her head. 'I won't be doing any writing any more,' she said.

He did not answer that. Instead he said, 'I have come to take you for a walk.'

'Me?' said Harriet.

'Yes. Along by the river. It is beautiful there in the evening. Nan says you can come. Come along, Harriet.'

'But—' Harriet sat up and put her legs down over the edge of the bed, 'don't you want to be with Bea?'

'No,' said Captain John, 'I want to be with you.'

They went downstairs together and out along the drive and past the jetty and along the footpath, that lay beside the river.

The up steamer and the down steamer, the mail steamers, had passed for the day and the river flowed calm and untroubled between its banks. Now under the bank it showed shallows of light, yellow, where the late sun struck down into it; further out the water was deeply green, and beyond, in midstream, it showed only a surface with flat pale colours. On the further bank, a mile across stream, there was a line of unbroken brilliant yellow above a line of white, the mustard fields in flower above the river's edge of sand. The temple showed its roof among the trees and country boats, their sails set square, moved gently down before the current and the wind. Other boats passed, towed upstream by boatmen leaning on long towing lines. A peasant was washing the flanks of his cows in the river above the garden, and on the sand and in the mud lay the halves of empty shells, bleached white, that had baked all day in the hot sun.

'How beautiful it is,' said Harriet. Its beauty penetrated into the heat and the ache of the hollowness inside her. It had a quiet unhurriedness, a time beat that was infinitely soothing to Harriet. 'You can't stop days or rivers,' not stop them, and not hurry them. Her cheeks grew cool and the ferment in her heart grew quieter too, more slow.

She was silent trying to think of it: then, 'I feel better already,' she said sadly.

'Don't you want to feel better?'

'No, I don't,' and she said with the same forlornness, 'I need some time to be unhappy.'

He did not answer, but he bent and took her hand, and holding his hand, she went on walking beside the river, her steps made a little jerky by his. His hand was very comforting to her.

'Soon – you will be going away though – won't you?' said Harriet.

'Yes,' said Captain John.

'What will you do? Do you know?'

'I don't know yet, but something.'

When the sun had gone, they turned and came back. Now the colours had drawn in to tints of themselves in the water and in the sky, but the mustard still showed its brilliant clashing yellow; the last clouds of the sunset hung over the temple. 'They are like cherubs' wings,' said Harriet. 'We always call them cherubs' wings.'

He made no answer to that.

They heard all the Indian evening sounds, sounds that were alien to him, utterly homely and familiar to Harriet: the gongs beating far off in the temple in the bazaar, the creak and knock of the ferryman's paddle as the ferry came near the bank; the sound of cooking pots being scoured with mud and of a calf bellowing while its mother was milked. There was an evening smell of cooking too, pungent, too raw for their noses with its ghee and garlic and mustard oil; there was the smell of dung fuel burning, and, as they came near the house again, they smelled the cork-tree flowers on the air.

'Those flowers are falling off the tree,' said Captain John.

'It is nearly the end of the cold weather, of the winter then,' said Harriet.

'I must go,' said Captain John, but he did not go. 'Harriet, will you come for another walk with me?' he said.

'Of course. Can we go for a walk when it is dark, and look at the fireflies? I have always wanted to do that,' said Harriet.

'Yes.' He still lingered. Then he said, 'Harry. Put your book back in its place. Promise.'

Harriet nodded.

'I like to think of it back in its place. And I am glad I am in it,' said Captain John.

*

As Harriet came into the nursery, where the lights were already on, Nan and Bea were kneeling on sheets of newspaper spread round Victoria's old basket cot. They were painting it with fresh white paint.

Harriet stood rooted to the threshold, staring.

'Goodness!' she said. 'My goodness!' And she asked startled, 'Is the baby coming then?'

They laughed at her startled face. 'Didn't you think it would?' asked Bea.

Harriet came slowly into the room, still staring.

'There,' said Nan, standing up and cleaning her brush in the jar of turpentine. 'That will be dry tomorrow. It is such excellent enamel,' she said with satisfaction. 'Look, it is nearly dry already.'

Harriet looked at Nan sharply. There was no sign in Nan's face of anything but satisfaction over the excellence of the enamel. 'Nan is like a clock,' said Harriet to herself. 'Every minute she ticks just that minute. Nothing else.' She said it irritably, but she sensed that all the other minutes were in Nan as well, a tremendous aggregate of minutes.

She said slowly, 'Nan, have you seen hundreds of babies born?'

'Not hundreds,' said Nan, 'but many. Very many.'

'And have you seen a great many people die?'

'Don't, Harriet,' said Bea sharply.

'But have you, Nan?'

'A great many, Harriet.'

'I don't understand,' said Harriet more slowly. 'I don't understand how you keep yourself so clear.'

'Don't you?' said Nan, but she did not tell them. 'I must go and see about your suppers,' she said.

After she had gone Harriet was left alone with Bea. Bea was still painting a leg of the cot, working the paint very carefully into the basketwork.

'Captain John has been so nice to me,' said Harriet.

'Has he?' said Bea.

'He took me for a walk.'

'Did he?' said Bea.

'He is – different, Bea.'

'Is he?'

Bea did not seem interested. She painted with small firm even strokes. Harriet could not see her face for her fall of hair.

'Bea,' said Harriet, 'are you unhappy?'

'Well, we all are,' said Bea, without looking up.

Harriet did not think it wise to continue, but she did. She could not go away.

'Does Captain John make you more unhappy, Bea?'

'No,' said Bea shortly.

'What do you do when you are unhappy?' asked Harriet.

'Oh, what a lot of questions you ask, Harriet. What is there to do? I am unhappy, that is all.'

She finished the leg and stood up and began to put her brush away with Nan's.

'I can't believe in this baby,' said Harriet, looking at the cot.

'It will be born all the same.'

'What happens, Bea?'

'Don't you remember when Victoria was born?'

All Harriet could remember was a story she had heard. When Victoria was born the head clerk of the Works, Sett Babu, came to Father and said, 'Sir, I hear you have another little calamity.' That was because Victoria was a girl and a girl to Sett Babu meant a dowry to be given when she was married. 'Do we have to have them?' she asked aloud.

'Have what? Babies?'

'Dowries,' said Harriet, but Bea did not answer.

'I don't see how we can,' said Harriet. 'How can we?'

'What? Have dowries?' asked Bea irritably.

'How can we be expected to have another baby and to like it? That is asking too much,' said Harriet. 'How *can* Mother?'

'If she is, she can. That is the answer,' said Bea. 'Harry, we ought to go and wash for supper.'

Harriet was silent, thinking, and then she said, 'It is too hard to be a person. You don't only have to go on and on. You have to be—' she looked for the word she needed and could not find it. Then, 'You have to be tall as well,' said Harriet.

In spite of the sadness and the quiet in the house there began to be a thread of expectation; then a stir.

The nurse came, Sister Silver, and Bea and Harriet were moved out of their room. Harriet went to sleep with Nan and Victoria; Bea went to stay with Valerie.

Then – will Captain John go there – to see her? thought Harriet. 'Won't he come here any more?' said Harriet.

An overwhelming loneliness filled her and the old misunderstood pain. She went again to the Secret Hole and again sat there by her soap-box, with her knees under her chin, brooding. Am I always going to be lonely? thought Harriet, and the right answer seemed to be, Yes, I expect I am.

She had kept her promise and put her book back and now she picked it up, but all the writing in it seemed broken and flat. How silly I was when I wrote it, thought Harriet. Valerie was right. It was all babyish and silly or else crude; the funny bits were not funny; the beautiful bits were too beautiful. 'I hate my writing,' said Harriet.

The day ends, the end begins.

She had not finished the poem. She looked at it. 'Nothing leaves off,' said Harriet crossly. 'But I shall leave off,' and she threw the book back in the box.

In the night she did not sleep well. She did not often sleep well now. Her dreams were too intimately concerned with Bogey, with the cobra. That night she woke in her customary cold sweat, and slowly, as she forced open her eyes, she saw that she had not woken to the frightening darkness when everything had long lithe shapes and might, or might not, be sliding, coming, moving, towards her. The light was on, and what had woken her was not a dream, but the sound of heavy treads. They came along the verandah and up the stairs past the nursery, and she heard a commonplace loud and cheerful voice, Dr Paget's voice. She lay and listened to it sleepily; then in a moment she sat up.

'Nan,' she said, 'is it the baby? Is the baby born?'

'Shsh,' said Nan's voice. 'You will wake Victoria.'

'Nan. What is—'

Harriet's voice stopped when she saw what Nan was doing. In front of a hot low brazier, Nan was airing the small clothes Harriet had often seen put away in Mother's trunk; Harriet looked dumbfounded. Washed, ironed and ready, a vest, a flannel nightgown, a coat, a white shawl, were airing there. 'It *is* the baby,' said Harriet in awe. 'The baby is going to come.'

Outside, in the night, a gong struck once.

Harriet listened. One. No more. It was the Works' gong, beaten at the hours. 'It is one o'clock in the middle of the night,' said Harriet. 'Is the baby born?'

'Not yet. Come,' said Nan. 'Get up. As you are awake. You shall help me make some tea.'

'Tea? Now? In the middle of the night?'

In the dining-room the tea things were laid out, sandwiches were cut. Harriet was astounded and Nan laughed at her face as she put on the kettle. 'Whom do you think I first put the kettle on for, here, in the middle of the night?' asked Nan.

'Who?'

'For you, Harriet.'

'For me?'

'Yes. You were born just after I came here.'

'And then – Bogey?'

'Then Bogey.' Nan said his name as if it were the same as anyone else's.

'Nan, you have seen so many babies,' said Harriet. 'Do they always seem new and exciting, like this, to you?'

'Always new,' said Nan, 'and exciting.'

'Every time?'

'Every time.'

Harriet pondered. 'But we don't want another boy, do we?' she said jealously.

'That isn't left to us,' said Nan. 'It won't be another anything. It will be itself.'

Sister Silver came down.

'Is the baby born?' asked Harriet.

'Why isn't that child in bed?' said Sister. 'Nurse, I think we shall want those clothes soon.'

'I am ready,' said Nan. She had poured out a cup of tea before she took up the tray. 'Now, Harriet, here is a cup of tea for you. Can I trust you not to wake Victoria?'

Harriet took her tea and went to sit by the brazier that shed a dim, warm circle of light in the nursery. Even the tea had a different flavour in the middle of the night, dark and strong and hot. It was too hot. She put the cup down and went to look out of the window.

The house was so warm and sheltered, so full of light and hush and life, that it did not know the night. At the window, Harriet met the chill of the early hours. There was no freshness in it yet, the dew had not fallen; the night was still strong. Far away, over and over again, she could hear the jackals howling and the two sounds, always present, always reminding her: puff-wait-puff, and the running of the river.

The strong night scent came to her again from the Lady-of-the-Night; it was heavy, more than ever drenching, in the dark. She did not like it. She shivered.

Usually now all of them in the family would have been asleep, like any sleeping family. She thought of all the families safely and unadventurously asleep and then of how her own was scattered. Only Victoria was in her place. Mother's room was out of bounds, she could not know what was happening to Mother; Father was awake, walking between the verandah and the drawing-room, she had heard him while Nan poured out tea. Bea was across the river and she herself was standing here tied with excitement so that she felt as if she had a knot in her stomach with the coldness of the night blowing on her forehead and the cold howling of the jackals in her ears. And Bogey . . . where was Bogey? The warm of him was gone. It didn't stay – it wasn't made blue by the cobra . . . then where . . . where? Harriet knew that it would be better, much better, not to think of Bogey now, in the middle of the night.

'If you are cold,' she told herself reasonably, 'why not drink your tea?' She went back to the heater and sat warming herself, her hands cold on the cup, her lips shivering as she drank. She could hear footsteps going backwards and forwards over her head in Mother's room.

Then she decided she would go out on the verandah and wait there. It was nearer. She could hear more clearly there.

The verandah showed her the night and now she saw the stars behind the cork tree, but the tree did not appear to be moving at all. 'But it is,' argued Harriet. 'It is, because it always does.' The scent of the night bush was softened here by the circle of cork-tree flowers, by the thin dew scent of Mother's petunias in the pots.

She is very quiet, thought Harriet. I thought people screamed and shrieked and cried when they had babies. She strained to hear and went to the foot of the stairs. No sound at all. Nothing. She began to walk upstairs.

It was dark on the centre landing, but the upper flight was lit and the lights were on outside Mother's room as well. Harriet kept in the shadow of the banisters. She could hear Father's steps, and cautiously she raised her head to look up. At that moment Sister Silver came out of Mother's room. She had her sleeves rolled, her face looked busy. As Harriet saw her, she saw Harriet.

'What are you doing up here?'

'Is it born?' asked Harriet.

'You go downstairs directly, Miss,' said Sister sharply, and Harriet retreated.

She did not retreat far, about nine steps. There she waited, and presently, when she judged it was safe, she came up again.

Then down the stairs a smell filtered to Harriet. She sniffed it. She knew it, and she had known what it was going to be. It was chloroform. She knew it from her operation for tonsils. There was no mistaking it. She came a little further up the stairs.

Nan was standing there outside Mother's door, but her back was turned to Harriet.

'Is it born?' That was on Harriet's tongue again when Nan's attitude arrested her.

Nan was standing and waiting for the moment to

come. The light showed her thin shoulder blades under the straps of her apron crossed on her back; it showed the combs holding her thin bun of hair, and her old black jacket that she wore under her apron, her print skirts, and slippers. As she stood there, she looked small and quiet and humble to Harriet, who felt she herself had been making something of a clamour. She felt ashamed, but not so ashamed that she went away. 'I couldn't, I couldn't go down now,' argued Harriet. 'Nobody could. Not now.' She stood, trying to emulate Nan in stillness, on the stairs.

Then Nan started, her hands unclasped, and a sound ran through Harriet from her scalp to her feet and from her feet up again.

It was a new sound. First it was a sound like birds chirping; like sparrows in twigs; a twig sound; then it grew; it was broken into hiccoughs: coughs; it was like a little engine starting; it grew again, and it was the baby crying. It was the actual baby crying.

There had never been any days as peaceful as those late winter days after the baby was born.

There was no ripple of disturbance in them. Mother lay in bed, and Harriet only saw her to say good morning and good night; Father was away, up-river, on a jute conference; Sister Silver lived apart with the baby and Mother; Bea was still with Valerie; Nan and Victoria were the only two with Harriet, and Nan was never a disturbance, and Victoria never, in any case, made ripples.

Now the days were tinged with heat at midday, cool again at morning and evening. It was almost spring. In the fields the early sowing was finished and the young jute and rice made dark-green and light-green patches over the land. The yellowness of the mustard had dimmed and the first great red pods of the simul, the wild cotton trees, had opened their colour. In the sky, the clouds were soft and puffed as cotton-wool. The sky itself had altered. This was the time of its deepest blue; later the heat took its colour, and later still the monsoon broke and turned it heavy and grey, with intervals that were pale, washed out. Now Harriet, by looking at the sky, knew it was nearly spring.

The sky so attracted her that she opened her money box and took out two annas and asked Ram Prasad to fetch her two new kites from the bazaar. He bought an excellent one, striped red and white with emerald corners, and a second one of plain pink paper. He helped Harriet to pierce the first, and fix it to her glassed string that was wound on a light polished roller made of bamboo with two long handles. Then they went up together on to the roof.

'You launch it,' said Ram Prasad, 'and I will get it up for you.'

'No. I want to get it up myself,' said Harriet.

'You never will. You never can.'

'I can. I shall,' said Harriet. 'Stand out of my way.'

She took the roller on the palms of her hands and allowed plenty of space behind her in which to run back. Ram Prasad took the kite between his fingers and walked with it to the other end of the roof.

Above them the sky waited for the kite. Nothing showed between the grey stone parapet walls, not a tree, not a roof, not a mast, except only the top of the cork tree flowering in its green, and, far up, the specks of the hawks making their circles on the edge of the wind current. 'I am going to send it as high as that,' said Harriet.

'Ready?' called Ram Prasad, holding it up.

'Ready.'

Ram Prasad sent it up in a strong flight. The string pulled taut, Harriet jerked it higher twice, the kite found the wind, rose and jerked away of itself in a short cornerwise dance. Harriet pulled backwards, it rose again, and then suddenly made an arc in the air and fell, dashing itself against the parapet.

'I told you so,' said Ram Prasad.

'Is it broken?'

She stood there while he looked at the torn kite. She kept her lips stiff. She meant to fly that kite. It was important to her that she should, because she had, in true Harriet fashion, made it into an omen. If it flies, I shall fly, is what Harriet had decided.

'It can be mended,' grunted Ram Prasad. As always when they sailed kites, he had brought the second kite up on the roof and with it a pot of flour-and-water paste, a stick with a rag round it and some strips of coloured paper. Squatting on their heels, he and Harriet began to mend the kite; they first patched the torn place, then they weighted the opposite tip with the same amount of paper and paste; they added a blob to the tail to steady it and laid the kite in the sun to dry.

Nowadays Ram Prasad and Harriet were neither of them conversational. While the kite dried Harriet went to lean over the parapet by herself, looking down on the garden as if it were a map in another focus. She saw a small launch tied to the jetty and a pigmy Captain John walking up the drive. She felt herself pause; she looked down on him, held in her thoughts. Then Ram Prasad called her. He held the roller. 'Pick up the kite,' he said, 'and I will get it up for you.'

'No,' said Harriet, 'I shall get it up for myself.'

'You will never do it.'

'Then it shall not be done,' said Harriet.

'If you have husband, poor Godforsaken man,' said Ram Prasad, 'he will need a padlock and a stick.'

'Put it up,' said Harriet, standing ready. She hoped she would get it well up before Captain John found out where they were.

Ram Prasad put it up, clumsily. Harriet stepped back, pulled, and the kite came down flat on the roof in front of her, flat on its back with its string doubled up.

'See how clever you are,' said Ram Prasad.

Harriet did not contradict him. 'Is it broken?' she said.

'No. No thanks to you, thanks to God.'

'Then put it up and more carefully this time.'

Her lips were in a firm straight line as Ram Prasad sent the kite into the sky. Captain John appeared in the stairway.

Harriet jerked her roller, the kite rode up; out of the corner of her eye she saw his eyes follow it. It rode up well, and she brought it up again strongly. Then she let it go a little and it danced away down the current of the wind.

'Bring it up,' said Ram Prasad.

'Leave me alone,' said Harriet.

She brought it up herself, riding straight again, then to the left, to the right, another cornerwise dance off, and a bold fresh flight taking the string. Now it was safe, right up riding the wind, taking the string out, further and further away, higher and higher.

'You do it well,' said Captain John.

'At the third try,' said Ram Prasad. 'Bogey Baba could get it up first time, every time.'

The kite string sang in the wind; it pulled and tugged at Harriet's hands ... 'This is me – me – me,' she was singing triumphantly to herself. The string seemed to go up until the kite was among the hawks' rings in the sky.

'Feel it,' she said, and put the roller into Captain John's hands.

It was handing him something that was alive. His arms jerked and his hands had to close quickly to hold it and he had to use his strength on it. She saw his cheeks flush and his eyes grow darker with the excitement of the kite. Soon she saw that he was nearly as moved and as exhilarated as she.

They flew the kite while the afternoon grew later and richer in the world beyond the parapet, until the small clouds took the sunset as they had on the walk by the river. The same sounds, the same smells, came up to them.

Now I have been up here long enough, thought Harriet. I am tired. She began to wind the kite in.

'Are you bringing it down?' he asked regretfully.

'Yes.' She added, 'I always like them to be in before the first star comes.'

'Why?'

'Because it would be fatal for them to be out then,' she said seriously. 'The star would turn them back into paper.'

He did not laugh as she had been half afraid he would. He gravely helped her to wind the string in and the kite came back to them, fluttering, pulling away, getting larger in the dusk until it was over their heads, and Ram Prasad put up his hands and caught it level with his turban, as the last wind sank out of its sides. 'That was not so bad,' said Ram Prasad, 'but not as well done as Bogey Baba could have done it.'

Captain John took Harriet downstairs to ask permission from Nan to go out. 'It is very late,' said Nan, looking at them over her spectacles. 'It is dark.'

'Yes, but we wanted it to be dark. I want to show Captain John the fireflies,' pleaded Harriet.

Nan appeared to be thinking it over. Harriet checked her own arguments, of which she had a torrent ready, and waited too.

'Very well,' said Nan at last. She wisely did not say anything about time, nor bed.

'Shall we say good night to the baby?' asked Harriet.

'Very well,' said Captain John.

The cot was on the verandah, and all they could see in the folds of shawl was the baby's head and face asleep, and her fist doubled up. As they looked, the shawl moved up and down with her breathing.

'Feel how warm she is,' said Harriet.

Captain John held his finger near.

'She is very ugly, isn't she?' said Harriet.

'Look again,' said Captain John.

Harriet looked, at the line of cheek and the forehead where the veins spread, at the tiny mottled lids, like seals or sleeping shells, that showed a line of hairs that were lashes. She saw the nose and the mouth whose corners folded as it slept, and the chin. 'There is a dimple in her chin, like Father's,' she whispered, and Captain John nodded. The lobe of the one ear Harriet could see was laid flat to the head with a glimpse of tender skin behind it, going into the line of the back of the head turned into the shawl. The head was covered with fluff, a down, that was gold too. Harriet looked at the doubled fist, and at the hand and the fingers and the nails. 'I like her nails,' said Harriet. And Mother made her, she thought, finished, complete outside and inside. That was the wonder. This, this like to like. That was the wonder: foals, little horses, to horses; rabbits to rabbits; people to people; all made without a mistake. And without a pattern, thought Harriet, touching the baby's hand. It was always a fresh shock to find it warm, soft and firm, the feel of a real hand ... Where did Mother ... what did Mother— she thought. Queer, what people can make: the flight of a kite – and poems – and babies. What a funny power – and I too, one day! thought Harriet, see, how I have grown already.

All at once she said to Captain John, 'Could I go just one minute? There is something I very badly want to write down.'

The minute was half an hour, but when Harriet came out of the Secret Hole, Captain John was waiting quietly for her.

It was nearly dark. They did not walk along the river.

'The villages are interesting at night,' said Harriet, 'and the fireflies are in the village tanks.' They walked away from the Works and the bazaar along the road, where it began to run through the fields and villages. Soon they came to a village. There was a stucco house on the edge of the huts, and, as they passed, a man whose white clothes shone in the darkness stepped through its gateway with a floating oil lamp in his hand. By this house there was an orange tree; it was in blossom like the cork tree, and its flowers glimmered as they passed it, and its scent followed them up the road.

'This is a very smelly time of year, isn't it?' said Harriet.

'You mean scented,' corrected Captain John.

'Yes. All the flowers smell,' said Harriet.

Here was a village tank, a sheet of water with a black shine, with the fireflies they had come to see along its bank and under its trees. Now they came to the huts built of earth, mud-walled with reed and bamboo roofs; every doorway, as they passed, was lit and showed a still life of figures or of things, lit and quiet. Here, on the earth floor, was a block of wood with a hollow in it, and a handful of spices and a pestle. 'That is where they grind spices for curry,' Harriet interpreted. By the block on the floor were chilis, bright red in the lamplight, and behind them on the wall hung a wicker scoop. 'That is for separating the husks from their rice,' said Harriet. Here a woman in a cotton cloth crouched down on her ankles, while she turned the stone handmill for grinding grain to flour; with her other hand she threw in the grain, and on her turning arm her silver bangle caught and lost the light. Two old men, next door, sat by the bamboo pole that held the roof up and shared a waterpipe, passing it from one to another politely. Here a mother sat and oiled another baby, her own baby, in her lap; the baby had a girdle of silver bells round its waist. There were sounds too of a tap, a goat bleating, of bullock-cart wheels in the road, of a passing bicycle's bell.

They went further, to another village and another, and then turned to come back. When they came to the first village again, some of the doorways were already dark, and the mother was singing to her baby, a song that was ineffably sleepy and low with only half cadences of notes.

'That is like Nan sings to our baby,' said Harriet. 'Nan sings like that.' The other woman was still grinding, the old men were still smoking and no one put the spices away.

From the stucco house, as they passed it, came music,

a flute, cymbals, the interpitched grasshopper-playing of a sitar, and a drum. As they came nearer, a man's voice began to sing.

'What is he singing?' asked Captain John.

Harriet listened, but she could not make out the words. 'It will be about Radha and Krishna, I expect, and their love. They are always singing about that. Or else about Ajunta and his wars. It is always love and war,' she said.

Now they had come back to the house again, and they went in at the gate and up the drive, where the cork tree stood in its complete wheel of fallen flowers. Its branches were quite bare.

'So the winter is over,' said Harriet, as they stood under it.

The drum gave two throbs, a beat, and was still. 'It has done, for tonight,' said Harriet. 'Do you remember Diwali, Captain John? There were drums there too.'

'Diwali?'

'The Feast of Lights.' He nodded. 'Funny,' said Harriet. 'We talked about living, and being born and dying, and we didn't now then about ... Bogey ... nor the baby really ... nor anything ...' And she said under her breath, '*Bellum ... Belli ... Bello ... Bello ... Amamus ...*

Amatis ... Amant. I was doing those then.' How young I was, thought Harriet. Now how I have grown, and she said aloud to Captain John, 'Are you any different?'

'I think I am,' said Captain John.

'Because you have decided to go?' asked Harriet.

'Partly, perhaps.'

Harriet nodded. 'That is what Nan used to say. "Leave him. He will go on when he is ready." I used to wonder what was wrong with you,' she said candidly. 'You hadn't died ... but ...'

'I wasn't alive?' he suggested.

'You hadn't come alive,' said Harriet, and she said, 'You were like the baby ... you had to be born ... You were quite right when you said that,' said Harriet. 'I died a bit ... with Bogey. I died much more when Valerie said that to me ... for a long time I didn't come alive ... not the whole afternoon!' she said.

'You are alive now, Harriet.'

'Yes, and so are you ...'

She had a sudden excess of happiness as she had had that other morning, long ago.

'Look at my tree,' she said. 'Do you see it turning ... Up in the stars? Sometimes,' she said, remembering that morning, 'I write poems that are taller than I am.'

Captain John brought his eyes down and looked at her. 'I thought you were not going to write any more.'

'That was—' but Harriet did not say what it was.

'You can't help it, can you?' said Captain John. 'And what is this one? A story? A poem?'

'It is a poem.'

'And I have to read it, don't I, Harriet?'

'It is too dark to read,' said Harriet.

'Well, say it to me then,' said Captain John.

'It is good enough to say,' said Harriet. 'Really it is. This one is good. You will enjoy it. You will really. I wrote it after my other poem. It is much older.'

'I see,' said Captain John.

'This is it,' said Harriet, and she said it aloud:

'*The day ends. The end begins . . .*'

'Hm!' said Captain John, when she had finished. 'You will be a real writer one day, Harriet.'

'Oh, yes,' said Harriet. 'I shall be very great and very very famous.'

He did not say anything to that and she ran her hand up and down the tree's smooth bark. The woodpeckers, of course, had gone to bed. 'Does everyone have one?' she asked.

'Have what? A poem?'

'No, a tree.'

'Not everyone finds theirs so soon,' said Captain John. 'You are lucky, Harriet. That is where I am going,' he said more firmly. 'I am going to look for mine.'

A launch, as it passed on the river, gave a mournful little hoot that sounded like an owl. A real owl hooted a minute after.

'I must go,' said Captain John.

'It is so dark you can hear the river,' said Harriet. She meant 'quiet', but dark was better. 'Time to go? Oh, no!' but that tag of remembrance came in her mind. When had she said it? You can't stop days or rivers?

Captain John smoothed his hair with his hand, smiled once more at Harriet, and went.

'But ... you haven't said goodbye to me,' she called, caught unawares, in dismay, but he did not answer and limped steadily away until his footsteps died in the distance, and she knew he had reached the Red House.

Slowly she turned the edge of the thick carpeted wheel of flowers over in the grass with her foot; over and over and over.

'Tomorrow we shall have to sweep these up,' said Harriet. 'They don't smell nice when they wither.'

She remembered something she had forgotten all these

days and weeks and months. She stepped over the old lily shoots up to the tree and put her hand down into the hollow she had found, all that time before. Cold, sticky from dew and tree-mould, her charm was still there.

My world, thought Harriet. She was pleased to have it again, but she thought regretfully, I have it still, but I never found out what it meant.

Holding it in her hand she went slowly across the drive and up the steps and into the house.

'Puff-wait-puff' sounded the escape steam from the Works, and the water ran calmly in the river.

RED DOE

They were riding down from the upper pastures to get Ibrahim married. He felt pleased and important. There was only one person whom Ibrahim, the son of Ali, the old herdsman, knew or felt anything about and that was Ibrahim; naturally the morning was pleasant and important to him.

It was so early, as they rode, that the grass in the valley far below showed in sheets of pale dew in the sun and the ice-streams shone, pale too, and bright with the early reflection of the sky; later in the day it, and they, would be a deep August blue and the grass would unroll, mile after mile, with the belts of coloured flowers that came in spring and summer; here spring was June, July, summer lasted a month, October brought the first snow and the rest of the year was winter; these were the high mountains of the north-west Himalayas that led into Ladakh or Little Tibet.

When the cavalcade of young men reined in to rest their ponies, whose legs shook from the steep way down, Ibrahim could feel and smell snow in the wind; it blew from the peaks that towered all round them on the skyline. Snow sometimes came in summer, 'But not today,' said Jassoof, Ibrahim's friend, laughing. 'You don't want frostbite today, eh, Ibrahim?' The mountains ringed the valley, their sides sheer of rock and slate and pumice, snow on their peaks, their gorges filled with rubble and ice, and the great, wide, brown-white glaciers crawling to the river. Ibrahim could see eagles flying in endless circles below the crags and he thought, watching them, It is windy there. He could hear the waterfalls that looked, from far away, like the crystals he found in the streams and sold in towns and villages on the way back to the plains.

Ibrahim's people were *bakriwars*, goatherd nomads who drove their flocks up every year to summer on this rich alpine grazing. They moved in clans, each with its elders. Ibrahim's clan had its encampment on an alp thousands of feet above the valley, in the last spruces of the forest where a small meadow spread its gentian and primulas and anemones and geums in the grass. Ibrahim did not notice flowers; they were part of the grass to him, grazing for his father's goats, as he did not see the colours of the glaciers, the wicked blue of the crevasses, the mountains or the snow-slopes of the passes; he only knew how many marches away each was, which led to fresh grazing grounds, which snow bridges would hold. If he saw the eagles it was only to judge the wind; deer were for hunting with spears, bears were to be avoided and the little wild marmots, who sat on their tails to scream at humans, were for him and his friends to throw stones at. Ibrahim knew goats and ponies; he did not count them as animals but as his life; he lived with them as he lived with his father, mother, uncles, cousins, friends, especially Jassoof; but they were themselves, he was Ibrahim; he was not responsible for them, he had nothing to bother him but now the time had come for him to have a wife.

'We want a good strong one,' his father had said. He had said that too of the Yarkandi pony they had bought last year. 'Not too young a girl, not less than fifteen, and strong.'

Ibrahim had nodded and felt a sudden curious tingling that seemed to come in his palms and his thighs and the backs of his knees, and his throat was suddenly parched. 'I want her to be beautiful,' he said.

'Beautiful!' cried his father shrilly. 'A beautiful woman is nothing but a nuisance. No, she must be strong, not too young and of good stock.'

'And beautiful,' said Ibrahim obstinately, and his father leant forward and slapped him on both cheeks. Ibrahim was a young cock among the youths of the clan but his father still slapped him when he thought it would do him good.

After that Ibrahim looked at every woman he saw, wondering if she were beautiful. They all looked beautiful in the distance but that was the way they walked, straight from heels to head, keeping themselves to themselves. Now Ibrahim's eyes came prying among them and he saw things he had not seen before: how their bare feet and ankles looked small under the folds of their black and red pleated trousers; how their black tunics swung out in skirts below their breasts, the full hems sewn and weighted with a load of white pearl buttons; how their veils hung loose but showed, under each, a flash of blue from the bracelet-size cap they wore on their heads; and how their silver jewellery sounded as they passed and repassed in and out of the huts and the tents, round the fires and through the flocks. Their anklets chinked, and their necklaces, and earrings; Ibrahim began to hear that chinking in his dreams.

When the clan marched the men drove the flocks, rode the ponies, and carried nothing unless it were a favourite child or a new-born kid. The women carried the gear of the camp on their heads, netted bundles of the heavy iron cooking-pots and platters; they carried their babies in slings, or a child on their hip; they dragged the dogs on strings and drove the slowly moving, sick, hurt animals. They were also often in childbirth; the caravan was always having to stop and wait for an hour or two, or even longer, while a woman gave birth. Then the Elders were pleased; they liked to see the caps and hoods of the children running about in the clan, but the young men were impatient, though they often had to do the same thing with the herds. Ibrahim looked and wondered; some of the women seemed to him beautiful, none of them beautiful enough.

Now the day had come and he and his cavalcade rode down through the forests which grew more and more balmy as they came lower in the valley. Here there was a noise of wild bees and of larks above the meadows, where the larch and spruce trees opened on small alps of grass heavy with clover. The air smelled of resin and of honey. Ibrahim sniffed it and, sniffing, he found, suddenly, that he could smell himself.

He had been given a new turban of bright blue muslin, and he wore the wedding blanket, dark blue with fringes and a scarlet border, but his homespun coat was his own because he had no other coat, and he smelled of wool and wood-smoke and sweat and goat. To smell himself made him feel more than ever full of Ibrahim and more and more he felt that tingling excitement.

The chief moment of his life, up to now, had been when his father had bought him a saddle, but it was not a new saddle, and it was used by his uncles and cousins as well as by his father and himself. It was the same when he was given his first full-size blanket, the homespun, hand-woven blanket-shawl that all the men carried like a plaid on their shoulders; the blanket was not Ibrahim's, it was family property.

Now the tall young Jassoof led a small pony with an empty pad. Ibrahim, and no one else, would lead it back and his wife, probably for the first and last time in her life, would ride beside him, back up the mountain to her new home and she would be his own, no one else would have the right to own her or use her except Ibrahim.

They were riding faster now that the path grew more gradual as it came near the valley. They rode like Cossacks on their small thick-set ponies, that were prized if they were short below the knee, well-shouldered, with thick necks and thick manes. The mares had their foals trotting loose after them. Manes and blanket-ends flew in the wind as they crossed the wooden bridge above the noise of the river, where it burst in thunder out of the mountain; the hooves of the ponies made an equal noise on the wood. Spray blew in their faces and excited them and Jassoof let out a cry, a whoop, that made the others whoop like demons or wild cats to answer him, and the ponies plunged and broke into a gallop that swept them into the valley, with the ground drumming under the galloping hooves. Then, at the far head of the valley, where a glacier spread and melted in streams across the grass, they saw a single dark speck, a hut.

Thick loud whoops came from every young man round Ibrahim, jokes cracked across him and they all began to whip their ponies. Ibrahim's grey kicked out, though he had not touched it, and broke away from the rest into a glade where mares and foals, running wild, were grazing on clover and forget-me-nots. Ibrahim knew he had seen the glade before; something else he had seen but he could not remember what; then it came into his mind that it had been when he was riding and that it had been exciting too, but another excitement. They had been hunting. Hunting? And then he remembered. It was a doe, a red doe, who had run, startled, out of the spruce trees, in front of them into this glade.

He remembered the shout that had gone up from the men and it seemed to him the same shout that was in his ears now; the whips had been lifted then too, and the ponies were lashed as they spread galloping, in a circle to head off the doe, while the older men, who had the spears, held them ready. Ibrahim had come up with the doe as she turned, driven back; he had come so close that he could see her red sides heaving for breath, her ears pressed down and her muzzle strained as she ran. Ibrahim had swung his pony on to her and she turned again but sideways, and the old man, his father, had thrown his spear, and she fell, pinned through the neck to the ground. It was Ibrahim who jumped from his saddle to cut her throat before she died.*

There was something else he could remember, that he

---

*Mahommedhans can only eat meat if the throat of the animal is cut while it is alive.

did not want to remember, and he reined in his pony and rode slowly, step by step, through the glade. He did not want to remember, but he did remember. He remembered himself bending down with the knife in his hand and he remembered, what he did not want to remember, that the doe, with blood gushing from her neck, had looked at him and then he was alone with her. No father, no Jassoof, no others were with him then; it was only Ibrahim and the doe, and he, her eyes knew, had done this to her. Suddenly, it was he who had been stricken, not the doe, because he was not Ibrahim, himself, any more, he was Ibrahim and the doe.

'Allah! Kill it!' shouted his father. 'Owl! It will be dead before you cut!' and, dazed, Ibrahim had taken his knife and killed her.

When she was dead she was dabbled with blood to her scut, her small pale tongue hung out with blood welling still from her mouth; her eyes slowly glazed, hiding their meaning, but all day he could not forget. Perhaps he had never forgotten but now, as his pony began to trot out of the glade, went into a canter, then to a gallop as it joined the others, he chuckled; he had remembered he had refused to eat the venison that night and that seemed to him, now, exceedingly funny.

They came to the hut. It stood by itself at the foot of the glacier on a fertile grazing plain fed by a hundred ice-springs. There were silver birch-trees and flowers; buffaloes and goats were grazing. Other huts and tents stood on the edge of the forest and everywhere the smoke from cooking fires was going up. Children stopped to watch these stranger men on their little horses as they splashed through the stream and rode in a circle round the hut, faster and faster with cat-calls and whoops, as the Elders and the men of the clan came out to meet them.

The feast began. Inside the hut, the fires were smoking and the men sat in a circle, dipping their hands into the iron bowls and platters of pilaff and roast kid and chapplattis and apricots stuffed with mutton, and curd and honey rice. Ibrahim, feeling young and oddly light and thin, was put in the place of honour between the Elders and he was grateful that he should be silent as became a young man. He was shy but he was also very hungry. The food was good and he ate until he felt his stomach expanding and his legs growing warm and well-being coming up his back into his neck and face, so that he began to smile, feeling jovial again and suitably old.

All the young men knew where the women were. There was a cloth stretched tightly across the hut, nailed from wall to wall, that kept bulging and swelling as bodies pressed against it and, from behind it, came a continual sound, whispering and giggling and laughing, and that soft chinking of jewellery. Ibrahim looked and felt more than ever warm and jovial. The tea bowls came round and the hookah, the water-pipe, with its gentle liquid bubbling sound passed from hand to hand. Ibrahim thought that, through the cloth, he had caught a gleam of scarlet; wedding clothes were scarlet trousers and tunic, with a dark veil and new cap and new jewellery that chinked, chinked, as Ibrahim had heard it in his dreams. She was young – he knew that because she had been born in the same year as himself, the year of the great snow – and she was sworn to be strong, but Ibrahim was thinking now of a woman's skin, and he knew that he had seen it without noticing, and he marvelled as he remembered how it was fine, soft, much softer and finer than his own; he thought of a woman's hair and knew he had seen it loosed, another woman hunting in it for vermin and combing it, long and blue-black in the sun; he thought of a woman's body, of his body and hers, hers soft where he was hard, hard where he was soft so that they matched, and he began to tingle and had to dig his nails into the backs of his knees as he sat.

The hookah went round and the bowls of tea; Ibrahim

thought they would sit there for ever and that it would never end. He took his turn at the pipe politely, he drank bowl after bowl of tea, he listened politely to the jokes, barbarous jokes that made the cloth shake; he smiled until he thought his cheeks would crack, and still it went on and on.

At last Jassoof stood up and now the time for politeness was over and the raw thing would be done. Now the Elders would lead out the girl and put her on the pony with the empty pad and Ibrahim would take its hair-rope in his hand and ride away with her.

There were no more jokes, no giggles; silence had fallen on the hut. The men separated into two dignified groups; the chief Elder, with his aged face and sorrel-dyed beard in the centre of his, Ibrahim in the centre of the other. Presents passed and the bride's dowry, a bundle of clothes, two good iron pots, and a few coins, were given to Jassoof; Jassoof's young brother stayed behind to drive up five chosen goats. Now the men went outside and the Elder went behind the cloth. Presently he came back and with him, supported on two sides by women, came Ibrahim's bride. All Ibrahim could see was a bundled shape in a red blanket, and the top of a bowed head. The blanket was wound to her nose, she kept her head obstinately down so that the edge of the blanket met her veil.

Ibrahim longed for her to look up until, looking round, he saw the same longing on the faces of all the men standing round. Some had wives at home, some were not yet married, but as they looked at the red bundle they had the same look, hot and thick and longing, and Ibrahim felt furiously angry and resentful; had she looked up then, he would have beaten her when they reached home.

She did not look up. With soft slow small steps, quite unlike her ordinary woman's stride, she went to the pony with the Elder, who lifted her on to the pad and put the rope into Ibrahim's hand. The women began to call out and laugh, a few to weep; the Elder stepped back and stood, tall and courteous, while the girl's father looked with expressionless eyes away to the mountains and Ibrahim's friends began to bit up their ponies and tighten their girths.

Jassoof had Ibrahim's grey pony. Ibrahim stood with the rope in his hand while the girl sat on the pad, motionless, her head down. As he stood there, he began to run his hand up and down the pony's neck, a cross impatient hand; he ran it up to the pad, down the neck to the head, up to the pad and then he noticed that every time his hand moved near the pad, the girl shrank back.

It amused him and he moved his hand more, brought it nearer her each time, nearer and nearer, so that first it touched her blanket, then the soft folds of her trousers and then, unexpectedly, warm and firm, her thigh. The round warmth and firmness of it astonished Ibrahim so much that at first he left his hand there through sheer surprise; an equally astonishing sweetness filled him, added to the warmth and thickness and longing, and then he felt her tremble. He felt her tremble and at that, triumphant strength filled him and he pressed his hand hard against her until something warm and wet fell on the back of his hand.

It was a tear.

Ibrahim stood still. The drop lay on the back of his hand; as he looked at it, it seemed that the Elder and the father and Jassoof and the young men and the women disappeared. Ibrahim was alone with this girl, sitting helpless on the pony, and he had made her cry. The trembling fear passed from her into him. He did not want to be married, he did not want to take her away, into his home and his hut and his bed and the days of his life, he did not want to have anything to do with such a business. He dropped the hair rope and turned away as the pony veered round.

The Elder caught the pony and courteously returned the rope to Ibrahim, showing no surprise. Jassoof caught his shoulder. 'Owl! Can't you hold your own wife?'

'I don't want a wife,' said Ibrahim.

'You will tonight,' said Jassoof.

Ibrahim mounted his pony and Jassoof pulled up the small pony beside him so that its nose touched Ibrahim s leg. A throng pressed round them and the calls and shouts sounded across the valley. Someone laid a whiplash across the ponies' tails and they started forward, jerking through the streams so that the riders were splashed knee high. Ibrahim saw the girl draw up her heels and her hands came out of the blanket and clutched the pad. They began to gallop over the grass, all filled, all comfortable and jovial, feeling themselves more men since the morning, pleasantly fillipped and excited. The married ones began to think of their wives, the young ones eyed Ibrahim's and wondered when their turn would come; gradually the feeling spread to Ibrahim. The girl sat hidden and inert but, under the blanket she was there, as warm and round and firm as the promise of her thigh, and presently he, Ibrahim, would undo that blanket.

He knew that, but he knew that he could not be only Ibrahim again; and, as they rode back into the red doe's glade, he knew that what had started in him with the doe was in him with the tear and would be in him now, for ever.

All the same he began to laugh as he led the way home.

THE LITTLE BLACK RAM

'You mother was a prostitute, the daughter of a prostitute!' The children called that after him, and the Elders
and the women cried, 'Shaitan! Seed of evil!' Jassoof did
not care; his father was dead, he had no mother, and his
tongue was so quick that he could give them worse abuse
than they gave him.

The clan prized courage, spirit and hardihood as they
prized endurance and strength, but they were gentle and
had the shepherd spirit; Jassoof, born one of them, was as
different as if he were differently coloured, a firebrand
with no sense of reason; he was a young thief, a bully,
noisy, quarrelsome and turbulent, against everyone with
everyone against him. 'What shall we do with him?'
sighed the Elders. Only Ezekiel, the oldest of them all,

thought something could be done. 'He will learn,' said Ezekiel.

'But when? When?' asked the exasperated Elders.

'Presently,' said Ezekiel. That did not solve the question of the fights among the boys when Jassoof was sent to help with the grazing, the upsets among the ponies when he was sent to drive with the men, the milk stolen from the buffaloes, the calves panic-stricken from his chasing when he was sent to keep the herd, the food stolen and the girls teased when he was left at home. Jassoof had no kinship with anything or anyone unless it were the clan's self-contained, self-reliant goats with their wicked yellow eyes and strong horns. '*Bhai*, Brother,' one of the boys might by accident call him in the warmth of play or work and he always retorted, 'I am not your brother. I have no brothers.'

Only, once, when he was lying on a rock, drumming his heels in the sun, putting back his head to feel the air on his face, shaking his black curls back from his short broad forehead to look up at the vault of the sky and dare the sun with his eyes, did he hear a sound that made him become suddenly still; it was a pipe that Mahmud had brought up from the plains and kept in his

waist knot and played to himself, a thin bamboo pipe.
As Mahmud played it, Jassoof could not bear it; it gave
him a feeling of piercing sadness and emptiness so that
he did not know what to do with himself; it made him
too much alone, a speck on the mountains, a nothing,
a grain among a million million grains; he wanted to go
and look into the face of another boy, to go near him if
it were only to kick him, or to clasp one of the great
goats round the neck even if it turned its horns on him.
Mahmud played on and the feeling swelled in Jassoof
until he felt he would crack in pieces with it and he
jumped down off the rock on Mahmud and began to
beat him.

'My pipe! My pipe!' Mahmud screamed, but the pipe
was crushed against the rock as they rolled over.
Mahmud's turban came off, Jassoof lay on Mahmud and
pommelled him, an elbow on his chest, his hand holding Mahmud's hair while the other fist drove unfairly
into his soft sides and belly. That made Jassoof feel
himself again and his eyes looked as wicked as the
goats'; when the other boys dragged him off, Mahmud
was half stunned and bleeding. 'You rascal! You good
for nothing! You young cock!' said Abdul Kharim, the
chief Elder, when Jassoof was sent for. Abdul Kharim

slapped him on both cheeks and ordered him to go on a five days' march with old Ezekiel, who, besides being the oldest, was the crossest man of the clan, to buy sheep and drive them back. 'Sheep?' said Jassoof in disgust.

'Sheep!' said Ezekiel. Jassoof thought that sheep did not please Ezekiel either.

The nomads seldom keep sheep; they breed small horses and buffaloes and goats, suited to movement and enduring the steep and difficult climbs of summer pasturing; sheep are too slow, too soft for this but, occasionally, just before the clans move down, the Elders will buy a few sheep to fatten and sell in the plains for the Indian autumn festivals. These were small fat-tailed sheep, prime for mutton and for wool; Ezekiel and Jassoof drove them back and, before the first day was over, Jassoof hated their soft woolly help-less bundled bodies and their bleating voices. 'Take care, young owl!' said Ezekiel, giving him a box on the ear. 'Would you have that ewe in the river?' Though his ear was tingling, Jassoof shrugged and scowled and then laughed scornfully; he would have put the whole flock in the river. Ezekiel gave him another blow to teach him manners.

Late that night the same bleating ewe was delivered of twin lambs; one of the lambs was black. 'Here, Shaitan, here's a brother for you at last,' said Ezekiel, lifting it.

The black lamb, still with its cord hanging, red and wet, its legs dangling, lay in Ezekiel's hand. It had barely drawn breath, but struggled fiercely to get away and tried to kick with its tiny hooves that were cloven and black. Its forehead, where the black curled hair was still sticky and damp from the birth was, indeed, very like Jassoof's but on its head it had the mark of embryo horns; it was a ram. 'Take it and keep it warm,' said Ezekiel, 'while I see to the mother. Warm the other one too.'

Jassoof picked up the white-grey lamb without interest but, when he put the black lamb under his coat and felt it move against him and butt him with its head, he was filled with a feeling that was the opposite of what he had experienced from Mahmud's pipe; he felt stirred, not to emptiness but, as he warmed the lamb, as if he were filled. When he felt its warmth, he felt the warmth of himself, Jassoof. He looked down at the small curled black head nuzzling in the rags of his coat and he was puzzled to find that this feeling was good.

After that he and the ram were inseparable. It was not,

Jassoof said, that he liked the ram but that it liked him; he pushed it away and even threw twigs and pebbles at it but it followed him where he went. It would not stay with the sheep but went after him among the goats and was not in the least afraid of them. It could balance on its small hooves as well as any of them; its legs grew as strong as springs, and its body grew hard. 'Allah! It will be tough eating,' said Ezekiel.

The boys teased Jassoof, which made him angry. When the clan moved back to the plains, they taunted him with the butcher. 'Butcher. Butcher will take your ram.' Jassoof half wanted the ram to go; the boys threw stones at it and that made another unaccustomed feeling rise up in him, though the throwing back of stones was customary enough. The thought of the ram stoned or slaughtered by the butcher made his stomach feel queer. He wished Abdul Kharim would order something quickly but in the end the Elder did not send the ram to be killed and, when the spring came and the flocks were driven back to the Himalayas, the ram was with them, trotting at Jassoof's heels. When it felt the mountain grass under its hooves and smelled the snow wind scented with honey from the flowers, it went wild with joy. It jumped with all four feet off the ground as it went cavorting and shying over the glades, shaking its neck and small fat tail with ecstasy. Jassoof suddenly laughed aloud, and in the same glee lay down and rolled in the flowers himself.

It grew large and strong; the hard small curves of its horns showed; and now, for the first time, Jassoof felt how troublesome the tiresomeness of another could be. On the strong mountain air and grass, the ram grew wicked; it would run at the women carrying their water-pots from the streams and raced among the children, sending them flying; the women clamoured for it to be killed or sent away. Abdul Kharim looked and heard and frowned, the boys threw more stones at it; everyone was against it and still it went bounding, kicking and butting round in the camp among the flocks, a small black tornado. 'Take that black devil away from the folds.' 'Aie! It has broken into the hut and eaten the fresh curd.' Then it ran at Rahman's Bibi when she was fully pregnant and she fell and had a premature birth; the baby lived but the anger broke out more fiercely. 'Slit its throat. It should be killed. Ill-begotten. Seed of evil. Shaitan!' The feeling rose in Jassoof again, mingled anger and queerness; the queerness was that he felt that he was no longer Jassoof alone, but Jassoof and the ram, and again it was like the feeling from

Mahmud's piping. He felt for it what he had not felt for himself, and he caught the ram by its neck and dragged it away from the camp to the goats. That night he did not go into the huts but slept out of doors with the goats and the ram.

Two days after that it ran at Daveed, a tall big sullen boy, almost a man, when he was riding an unbroken colt, which swerved in fright, throwing Daveed; even the women laughed while Daveed scowled, picked up a stone and hurled it in temper at the ram. The stone, too large to throw at an animal, broke the ram's leg.

When any animal in the herd broke a leg, they sent for Ezekiel. If it were a clean break he, with his old clever hands, would delicately set it, splint it, and hold the splint in position with a crisscross network of light twigs tightly bound up the flank so that the whole limb was held stiffly when the animal moved; it was skilled work and took a long time. Now Ezekiel came and looked at the black ram. Jassoof felt himself tremble; no one liked the ram, they all wished it dead. Would Ezekiel cut its throat? 'It's a clean break,' said Jassoof and his tongue came out and licked his dry lips. Why could he not say a simple thing like that without his tongue becoming dry and his heart beating?

Ezekiel grunted.

'It would not be . . . difficult?' asked Jassoof. The ram lay with its sides heaving in pain, moisture running from its nose. There was silence, till Ezekiel grunted again and, squatting down on his ankles, took twine out of the deep pocket of his homespun coat and began to work. He sent a boy for twigs and told Jassoof to hold the ram. 'You are my father and mother,' said Jassoof humbly.

The ram kicked hard with the other leg as Ezekiel pulled its broken leg straight. 'Inshallah!' cried Ezekiel and swore at Jassoof for not holding it better. The boy pleaded under his breath with the ram to lie still, for he was afraid Ezekiel might grow cross and leave it but now he saw what patience the old man had; it is animal nature to kick and struggle against forcible pain and the ram struggled wildly but Ezekiel went steadily on till the leg was straight in the splints and the network, woven with twigs and tied with twine, was so firm that even the most energetic ram could not kick it off. A reverence for Ezekiel began in Jassoof, who had never felt reverence for anything or anybody before; Ezekiel was taciturn and cross but had this power of healing which he would use for a bad boy and a plaguey young ram. When at last the ram was released it scrabbled with its feet on the ground and quivered, blew through its nostrils and stood upright. 'In three weeks it will mend,' said Ezekiel, dusting his hands.

'God is great!' said Jassoof politely; his eyes glowed; at that moment he thought Ezekiel greater than God.

It was four days later that Abdul Kharim ordered that the clan should move, crossing the high passes that led down to the valley of the Liddar on the other side of the great range. 'It is too late in the season,' grumbled Ezekiel. 'It is mad! The last pass is one of the worst in the mountains. If we get snow, there will be death. His father would not have done it.'

They left the huts standing under the trees and began their march through the gorges and up the mountains to the passes. Day after day they journeyed on, passing rivers of water and rivers of ice, great glaciers perpetually frozen; climbing crags and precipices, wandering across high unknown glades, making a new camp each night, stopping sometimes for an hour or two for the birth of a child or of a late calf.

Jassoof, as he had the lame ram, was given the task of driving all the sick animals; usually only a woman or the mildest of the boys had patience to do this but now the fierce Jassoof left camp first in the morning and came in late, long after the others, sometimes long after dark. He had an old she-goat, once the leader of her flock, huge, old, tufted, ugly and maddeningly obstinate; with her was a spotted half-grown goat as disobedient as she, and a small fat kid he had to carry. They all had broken legs, splinted like the ram's and they walked, limping and hopping, stopping and whimpering, trying to lie down or break away. Only the black ram limped faithfully behind Jassoof and that made Jassoof go on and not rebel though it seemed to him that each day was a moon of days; he lashed the old she-goat unmercifully but brought them all safely into camp each night. 'That is a changed boy,' said Abdul Kharim.

'I told you he would learn,' said Ezekiel, smoothing his beard. Then he added, 'But he will have to learn to do without the ram.'

'But it is with the ram that he is good.'

'He will learn to do without the ram,' said Ezekiel. 'One day he will have to learn.'

They camped one evening not far from the foot of the last pass; its crags loomed over them and the night was cold, without stars. 'Snow,' said Ezekiel, sniffing the air. 'I told them! Snow!'

Next day, they were early on the march and Jassoof was

soon left behind. That morning the old she-goat seemed possessed of the devil and the young goat followed her; it was not till long after mid-day that Jassoof drove them, dragging the kid in his arms, up among the rocks at the foot of the long cleft that led up to the pass.

He stood and looked at it, putting his head far back. It towered for hundreds of feet over his head, sheer rock in which the wind, ice and water had hollowed a curious funnel up which it was possible to climb on a spiral stair of great toothed rocks; it was steep and wildly rough. Eleven young men, with shouts and cries, were shouldering a buffalo up it; the buffalo panicked and lowed, but up it went, while the rocks gave the echoes back. The whole air round was filled with lowing and bleating and cries; there was pandemonium at the foot of the cleft; women were weeping; men sweated and swore, dragging and beating the animals. The boys were carrying up the kids on their necks; the goats went neatly their own way, but the buffaloes had to be pushed and lifted and the ponies swung by necks and tails from rock to rock. Slowly the crowd thinned and, from far up and out of sight, bleating and whistles dropped through the air and faded out of hearing.

As the afternoon went on, the light changed and

flakes of snow began to fall; the flakes grew heavier and the work became feverish. Women, young men and boys went up and down, up and down. Jassoof left his sick ones grazing and worked, carrying kids, pots and bundles until his legs and back ached. One by one the other boys left and went on with the flocks, but Jassoof had always to return to his hurt animals. He knew they must be the last.

When most had gone he took up the kid and gave it to another boy to carry while he came back for the half-grown spotted goat; but the step from rock to rock was too high for him to manage with its weight and if he dumped it on each rock ahead of him, it came down too hard on its injured leg. The men swore at him to keep out of the way and crestfallen he brought the goat back and waited. At last only he, two goats, the ram and a pair of small white ponies were left. The snow was now falling so fast that Jassoof wondered what it would be like up on the head of the pass. 'If it is a blizzard . . . Aie!' He rubbed his hands inside his knees and chafed his bare ankles trying to keep warm, waiting for someone to come back. The animals quietly cropped the grass with the snow falling on their coats.

At last he heard men coming. There were four of them

with the young Daveed. Jassoof sprang to his feet to help them. 'It's big snow,' they called to him and they started with the ponies, two men to each. 'Hurry! Everyone has gone,' they called. 'We shan't get over if we are not quick. Quick. Hurry.' Daveed swung the young spotted goat up on his shoulders. 'Hurry. Come along, fool! What are you standing there for? Hurry. Be quick.'

'But ... these,' cried Jassoof for the old she-goat and ram.

'We won't wait for those. They are no good. She is old and he is Shaitan.'

'But ...' cried Jassoof running towards them. 'They can't come alone.' The ram, as it always did, came after him to see, butting him aside with its head.

'Leave them,' called the men. 'All that can't run are to be left. Hurry! Hurry!'

Jassoof's cry followed them. 'I have brought them so far.

'Turn them loose. Hurry.'

'Come down again. Come back for us,' called Jassoof.

One of the men turned round. 'Little fool. You must save your own skin. Come on.'

'Brother ...'

Daveed's voice called back, mocking, 'I have no brother.'

Jassoof cried, 'For the love of God ...'

Nobody answered him.

Soon, far above, the voices and shouts died away. The quiet was eerie where the noise had been. The snow fell and the light dimmed to twilight. The old she-goat went back to her greedy cropping but the ram stayed by Jassoof; it was cold and wanted his warmth, its breath steamed over his hand. 'Inshallah!' muttered Jassoof, bending to pick up the ram.

Its weight for him was tremendous, far more than the weight of the young goat. He staggered with it to the first rock and across to the second, but his arms were torn almost from their sockets while his heart felt as if it would burst his chest. On the third rock he had to dump the ram and he felt the jar as its leg met the rock and heard its sudden surprised hurt bleat. 'Nahin!' said Jassoof and set his teeth and struggled up with it once more and managed to get it safely to the next rock, but the sides of the funnel and the snow were whirling dizzily round him and he had to sit down and put his head on his knees. 'And there are fifty rocks to get up, fifty, seventy, a hundred.' Jassoof could not count but he remembered the rocks leading up. The snow was coming thicker, blown in gusts and eddies, whirling in his face

and choking him and it was not twilight now but getting dark. He could hear the old she-goat bleating; she
knew that she was left. He sank his head down on his
knees again.

'Ja-a-soof!'

'Yé. Yé,' called Jassoof, springing up. 'Yé. Come down!
Come down! There is one more. Come down.'

'Come up,' called the voice. 'Hurry. Little fool. Come
up. You will be lost,' called the voice. 'You will break your
neck.'

'Come d-own,' called Jassoof.

'Come up. Come up. Come up.' He could hear the
voice going away. 'Co-me u-p, Ja-a-soo-oof . . .'

All that he could see of the ram was a bulky blackness
by his side, but he could feel it warm and close. He bent
and with another effort picked it up again. Holding it
against him for a moment he looked up, then turned
back, struggling, slipping, dashing his feet against the
stones, bruising his elbows and knees, he got it back to
the foot of the cleft; there, sobbing for breath, he lay
down, curled, letting the snow beat down on him lying
still with the ram in his arms, but the animal did not
understand and indignantly broke away, struggled and got
up, bleating.

It was senseless to lie there alone. He stood up, a great fear sweeping over him. Numbed with cold, he shook his legs and shoulders, while the snow blew in his eyes and mouth. He looked up at the cleft again. There, somewhere ahead, if he could catch up with them, were his people, warmth and food. The she-goat had come back and stood with the ram looking at him and waiting.

Slowly, Jassoof unwound his short turban from his head and slowly wound it on again, winding the cloth over his head and ears, round his neck and over his mouth. The she-goat and the ram still stood waiting. Jassoof gulped and turned towards the cleft.

The old goat remained where she was but the ram at once hopped and scrambled after him. He heard it bleating as it tried to get up on the first rock; its hooves scrabbled as it fell back. It bleated. Jassoof went on up the cleft. The bleating followed him a little way, then he could hear it no more.

Alone, he went up the cleft as easily and quickly as any strong young goat; the snow gusts hit him without hurting him, but he had another pain; almost breaking him was that same piercing emptiness and sadness that had come from Mahmud's pipe. There was nothing to break now but himself; the ram was gone.

As he found the top of the pass he came out on a level cliff of rock and began to run towards the track that led down through the gathering darkness. The feeling grew until he felt he must break and then there was a strange relief as he felt something on his face, drops of something warm and wet that appeared to come out of himself, out of that aching pain; strange drops, for when they were on his cheeks they froze to ice though when they came out of his eyes they were fresh and warm. As he ran towards the path they came faster, till they prevented him from running. He stood still while his tears fell fast.